The boy who taught the beekeeper to read

SUSAN HILL

Chatto & Windus
LONDON

Published by Chatto & Windus 2003

2 4 6 8 10 9 7 5 3 1

This collection © Susan Hill 2003

First published in Great Britain in 2003 by
Chatto & Windus
Random House, 20 Vauxhall Bridge Road,
London SW1V 2SA

Random House Australia (Pty) Limited
20 Alfred Street, Milsons Point, Sydney,
New South Wales 2061, Australia

Random House New Zealand Limited
18 Poland Road, Glenfield,
Auckland 10, New Zealand

Random House South Africa (Pty) Limited
Endulini, 5A Jubilee Road, Parktown 2193, South Africa

The Random House Group Limited Reg. No. 954009
www.randomhouse.co.uk

A CIP catalogue record for this book
is available from the British Library

ISBN 0 7011 7596 6

Papers used by Random House are natural,
recyclable products made from wood grown in sustainable forests;
the manufacturing processes conform to the environmental
regulations of the country of origin.

Typeset by Deltatype Ltd, Birkenhead, Merseyside

Printed and bound in Great Britain by
Mackays of Chatham PLC

Contents

To Vivien Green
Best of Agents

*The boy who
taught the beekeeper to read*

The boy who
taught the beekeeper to read

'What are you doing?'

There might be a boldness in the boy's voice but there was fear in his heart too and the boldness hardly concealed it. Mart May could tell.

He had emerged out of the shimmering white gold of the mid-afternoon high summer garden into the deep green cool, a thin boy with arms and legs as greenish pale as peeled twigs, pale hair; but he stood his ground, once upon it, which Mart admired.

'Listen,' he said.

The small boy stared.

'Go on — you listen.'

They both stood quite still, the man in the strange helmet and ghostly garment and the stick-limbed boy. There was no movement of air among the dark heavy August leaves, so that the vibrating in the branches of the oak tree above them was clearly heard, like the sweet music of comb and paper.

'What is singing?'

'The swarm.'

'Oh.'

After a moment Mart May said, 'You visiting?'

'I came last night. It was dark.'

'On holiday then.'

The boy seemed to consider it, but in the end did not reply.

Mart May bunched the ankles of the billowing white suit into bicycle clips. The boy went on watching.

'You could hold the ladder,' Mart said, 'see I don't come a purler.'

'What is that?'

'A purler? Where've you been all your life?'

'In Scotland and London and Kent and France and London.' He ticked the places off.

Something about the careful answer, and about the seriousness of the pale boy's pale face touched Mart May at a level he scarcely knew in himself. He felt it as a swift sharp twisting sensation in his throat.

The boy wore long shorts, almost to the knee, and a cotton shirt with a neat collar.

'A purler,' Mart May said at last, 'is a tumble-fall. I don't want to climb that tree and have the ladder slip.'

'What would you have done if I hadn't come?'

'Mind out for myself like I always do.'

'Why are you going up the ladder?'

'To take the swarm.'

'Where?'

'Back to the hive where they ought to be.'

'Are they your bees?'

'They say a swarm belongs to you until it's out of sight and then it's anybody's. They're her ladyship's bees. I look after them.'

He lifted the ladder and propped it against the tree directly below the widest spreading branch. The boy waited until it was wedged in place and then came forward and put his hands on either side. Mart May climbed delicately, effortlessly; the swarm of bees was taken into the cotton bag and carried like burglary swag down to the ground and across the clearing on the far side of the glade. The boy followed, silent, watching, his green-white body a small ghost behind the voluminous billowing beekeeper.

'What will happen now?'

'They'll settle down. Takes a while.'

'They didn't sting you.'

'Their bellies were full. When they're that way they can't bend themselves to sting.'

'Why did you wear your covering-up thing?'

'Best be on the safe side.'

'When do they sting you?'

'When something upsets them.'

'What will upset them?'

'This and that. Losing their queen. People getting in their path. Thunder.'

Mart May the man began to emerge from the suit like a grub from a chrysalis. He folded the discarded white husk and set the helmet on top. A low soft hum came from the beehive.

The boy stood in the underwater light of the clearing. Beyond, the shimmering garden. Mart May opened his mouth to ask his name but the boy slipped through the hair crack between the forming of the words and their speaking and was gone, absorbed into the sunlight, leaving the bee man heavy among the shadows.

The hot weather settled in. The garden was drenched with butterflies and the petals floating off the last of the roses. Behind the garden the house remained half-shuttered the whole of each day. When Mart May was sent for to smoke out a wasp's nest in the attics he made his way through ocean depths of corridor, but the attic was hot as a boiler room and baking in the sun. Long-dead spiders were caught, transparent in dirty webs.

'What are you doing?' The boy watched him emerging silently as if through the wall.

'Smoking out the jaspers.'

For the first time he laughed. '*Jaspers.*'

'Wasps to you, then. And if bees won't go for you, these will. You steer clear.'

'I'm not afraid.'

'Well, I am afraid for my job if I let them pepper you.'

Mart May waited for the boy to move to the farthest end of the baking attic before pumping out the smoke.

Like a white moth the boy pressed himself against the wall and watched.

'Now we scram,' Mart May said after a moment.

They stood on the landing outside letting their eyes adjust to the dimness.

'I thought you were the bee man.'

'So I am, and a lot else besides.'

'Wasp man.'

'Window cleaner, guttering clearer, rabbit popper, boiler stoker, pigeon shooter, rat catcher, molehill flattener, leaf sweeper and a few I've forgotten for now.'

'My mother is dead so I came here.'

The dust surrounding them on the landing stopped seething, like the stopping of a clock.

'What's your name?'

'Mart May.'

He was gone again, quicksilver down the steep dark stairs. Mart stood, hearing the faint far-off closing of a door, and then the silence again, like felt in his ears.

After that, they met several times a week, the boy materialising wherever Mart May happened to be working, so that it seemed he had been waiting, following.

The name, he said, was James Burnett. But he was never anything to Mart but 'the boy'.

'My father is working in a dangerous country. I'm not allowed to go.'

'Well you're safe enough here if you steer clear of jaspers and don't fall in the pond.'

'I can swim.'

'All the same.'

'If I drowned, would you lose your job?'

'Very like.'

'Likely.' His voice was clear as a flute, and prim as a girl's.

'What, you being my schoolmarm now? You'd have a job on.'

Mart May was scraping the last of the honey from the combs. The boy, as always, watching, watching. Close up, even his eyelashes were pale, feathers above cloud-grey eyes.

'You like this?' He held out the comb. 'Make your hair curl.'

'That's bread crusts. My father won't come home for at least a year.'

'He won't know you then.'

The cloud eyes flickered with alarm.

'All that bread crust and honey'll have made your hair gone curlified.'

'*Curlified.*'

'That's it.'

9

'How do you spell "curlified"?'

Mart May rested the cleaned comb on the tray. In the lance of sunlight falling between the leaves, the gnats danced.

'Her ladyship would be your grandmother then?' he said at last.

'No, my aunt. Don't you know?'

'I do now. You've told me.'

'Not that. Don't you know how to spell "curlified"?'

'No,' Mart May said, walking away, 'I don't.'

When he glanced round the boy had gone.

He did not appear again for three days. The weather turned warm and sultry, there was no air, no stirring of the leaves. The bees teemed inside the hives, restless, pent-up, sullen.

Once or twice Mart May caught sight of Lady Burnett walking slowly along the gravel path, pulling off the dead heads of a late rose here and there, probing the dahlias with her stick. She kept aware. Hayes the gardener dealt with her, took the orders, heard the complaints. She never came into the glade, though occasionally when he was doing some job about the house she came upon him, and always spoke. Polite, haughty.

'What's that?'

The boy slipped into sight from behind the old stables. Mart May was sitting astride the old mounting block.

'A blade. It got warped – see – ?' He held out the bent metal.

'Can you flatten it?'

'Should do.'

There had not been horses here for years. The stables were used for storage, but the tack-room was Mart May's, where he brewed tea, ate his sandwiches, had an old radio.

'I saw a lot of jaspers, going in and out of a hole.'

'Where was that?'

'By the tomato greenhouse.'

'Right. We'll go along in a bit and do for 'em.'

'*Do for 'em.*'

'And don't you ever go poking into their nests with a stick or such.'

'Would they turn nasty?'

'Mad as mad. You leave them to me. Just report back.'

'Report back.'

'Little Sir Echo.'

'I like the things you say and how you say them. I like to say them as well.'

Mart May held out the blade. 'Nearly there.'

'What's it for?'

'Hacksaw.'

The boy swung the tack-room door gently to and fro.

'You see in there – the old cupboard on the wall?'

'"First Aid",' the boy read. 'The letters are nearly worn off.'

'The one with the cross on. Open it and you'll find a tin.'

'There are quite a few tins.'

'A tin with some writing.'

'Does it say "National Dried Milk"?'

'A silver tin.'

'Does it?'

'Open it. If it's got mints in it does.'

'Oh –'

'Have one. Keep your mouth watered.'

'You must like mints a lot. Mint toffees. Mintoes. Mint humbugs. Mint Imperials. Extra Strong Mints.' The boy ferreted about amongst the cellophane.

'You can get me out an Imperial, if you please.'

They sat, Mart May on the block, the boy on the broken-backed chair, turning the sweets around and around in their mouths.

The late swallows skimmed low into the doorway of the end stable and out again.

'Pity you don't have a pal to play with. Bit lonely, here with the old people.'

'I haven't got a pal.'

'Must have.'

'No.'

'You'd better get looking.'

'I'm going to a new school.'

'You'll get pals there then.'

'Will I?'

Mart May looked up. The boy's pale face was troubled.

'You'll be bringing 'em here soon enough, plaguing me, going off to their places, plaguing.'

'Plaguing.'

'Still, bit of life about the place is a good thing.'

'Were there horses?'

'Long before I got here.'

'When did you get here?'

'Fifteen-sixteen year. Right.' He swung himself off the block, holding the blade.

'Can I have another mint?'

'And put the tin back after.'

'Is it your tin?'

'It is now.'

'You should have your name on it, then. Mart May. At school you have to have your name on everything, every single thing.'

'School's a nest of thieves, then, is it?'

'"A nest of thieves". Why a nest?'

Mart May walked off, slowly, carrying the blade. 'You,' he said, 'make my head buzz.'

The boy made a boil in his cheek with the mint and put the tin back in the cupboard.

Mart May was in the toolshed fitting the blade into the hacksaw.

'If you had a brush and some paint I could do it for you.'

'Do what?'

'Paint your name on the tin.'

'Get on, there's no thieves here.'

The boy rubbed the toe of his sandal to and fro in the dry earth, making it fly up like sand. Mart May laughed. 'I suppose if I don't let you you'll burst open.'

'I will paint your name on the tin and on the cupboard and on the door and on this door.'

'You'll not, these belong to her ladyship. Just the tin. There's some old paint back of that shelf if it isn't all dried up.'

The boy had seemed odd, solemn, quiet, pale, not like any boy he'd ever encountered, but now, clambering down with the paint tin and beetling off across the yard, he was changed, excited, full of what he was doing. Ordinary, Mart May thought. Normal. He wants to be normal. Just wanted the chance, he thought.

He had no children.

He bent his head and back to sawing.

After a couple of minutes the boy was back at his elbow. 'Is it M-A-Y or M-E-Y?'

The saw froze. Mart May looked at the golden dust in soft heaps at his feet.

'Mart May? Which is it?'

He looked straight into the boy's sea-green eyes.
Saw a fleck of green, there, like a wand drawn across.

The boy waited.

'I can't say I know,' the man said quietly, rubbing
his finger up and down on the flat of the jaw.

'You have to know.'

'Well, I haven't, because I don't.'

The sea-green eyes widened. 'Mart May?' There
was a strange awe in the boy's voice. 'Can you not
spell?'

'I cannot.'

'Can you not write?'

'I cannot.'

The boy struggled for several seconds with this
astonishing, unprecedented truth.

'Can you not – *read*?'

Mart May stood his ground and held his gaze. 'No,'
he said calmly, 'I cannot.'

The boy let out a soft slow breath, a sigh of
wonder through pursed lips. 'I think it would be
good,' he said at last, 'if you learned.'

Mart May laughed, discomforted. 'You think I
should go back to school, then?'

'Oh no.' The boy did not laugh. 'I shall teach you.'

A week passed. Every day, the boy waited, carrying two books and two pencils, and every day Mart May was busy. Seeing the books and pencils made him sweat. The old anxieties which he had thought long dead pulsed in the pit of his stomach. He hid, found jobs in distant outbuildings and fields, but always the boy discovered him, as if by some magic sense, and materialised behind or beside him with the two books, the two pencils.

The sullen weather pressed in. The sun was sulphurous. The leaves hung heavy. The bees fumed.

'We should start,' the boy said, sliding into the tack room. Behind his small pale figure the clouds were gathering, curdled, inky. Mart May had switched on the light, a single bulb strung to the beam above.

He was plaiting onions.

'Your aunt doesn't pay me to look at picture books.'

The boy had pulled a stool up to the workbench under the dirty window. The two books and two pencils were set between them.

Panic flustered the man. Words bubbled up, excuses, fears, but remained foaming in his mouth.

Thunder rumbled in the distance. The boy opened

the books. At once, black letters danced malignly before Mart May's eyes, evil, spiked, terrifying marks, blurring together, separating, making his head sore. He began to breathe too quickly.

'First we find the letters of your name. M.' The boy pointed. Mart May stared as the marks swerved, leaned, straightened themselves again.

'M.'

Under the boy's small finger, the marks became still. The nail was like a shell, the blood flushed rose-pink beneath it.

'Now you find "M".'

The rain began, single drops plashing fatly onto the roof. Thunder grumbled.

The boy's neck and ears were like doeskin.

Slowly Mart May set his own thick, dirty forefinger on the page and moved it along between the forest of letters. The boy watched.

'M.' The finger swatted the fly-black letter, crushing it.

'Good.'

Mart May felt a flush of pleasure swell in him.

'A is the next. "M-A",' and the small finger set off

again moving confidently over the paper. It rested on a letter like a tripod.

The shed was livid with lightning, and the roof erupted under the battering of the rain.

Every day he returned, carrying the two books, the two pencils and every day Mart May could do no other than sit down somewhere – up to the bench, in the attic, on the window ledge, on the mounting block – and follow the small finger, stumbling his way along the black trails. After that the boy made him write the letters he had read. His small pale face was intent, his body willing Mart May on.

The summer days flamed into one another without rain after the single storm which had not lightened the air. In the still clammy nights the black letters took on life, crackled and became barbed wire, sharp with some terrible inner electricity zapping through Mart May's dreams.

Relentlessly each morning and afternoon, the boy slid up beside him.

'M-A-R-T M-A-Y.'

The man wrote line after line of penance, detained in the shed, the tack room, the hot attic.

'M-A-R-T M-A-Y. M-A-R-T M-A-Y.'

'You can do it. You can. Tomorrow I'm going to teach you my name.'

But on that next day, for the first time in nine years, the man did not go to work. His head was stabbed with black spikes. For a week he did not go. He was exhausted by a fear within him which formed itself into a dread of seeing the boy.

He sat in the dim kitchen. The light from the small panes filtered through the plants that filled the window ledge and clambered up from the flower bed outside. The room smelled permanently, faintly, of cat. He slept half the day, but the dreams had eased. The black letters became velvet and fur, blurred and softened at the edges.

At last, he woke to rain, soft veils of it blotting out the colour from the sky. He took his bicycle from the lean-to and rode to the bees.

It was as though he had slept for a year and woken in shame to see what he had neglected. For the four days he worked until late into the evening, as if to do penance. He felt changed, older, was uncomfortable inside his own skin, uncertain where he had always known certainty.

Late on the fourth afternoon, coming into the tack room, he saw that the catch was off on the door of the wall cupboard. It swung open to his touch. The silver tin with the worn blue letters was at the front. He lifted it down, opened it, took out a mint, and, as the fumes of it caught his throat, he had a sudden sharp sense of loss and emptiness. The boy had not appeared once since his return.

Three more days passed, during which Mart May felt restless, missing the quiet, pale figure at his elbow. He wanted to ask about him, but did not, only worked on at this job or that, until gradually he was no longer so alert for the sudden appearances. Days were like the old days again and beginning to shorten. The bees were still and close. The evenings and nights were cool.

He should have been settled in himself as the year slipped down, his old self, but he lacked something and there was always an edge to his mood, a frustration. He had unfinished business.

He spoke sometimes to the bees.

In the middle of an afternoon he finished repairing the hinge on the gate into the sunken garden, swung it to and fro to see that it ran smooth, and then, as if hearing a click in his head, at the same time as the latch clicked shut he knew what he should do.

In the shed, at the back of the shelf, he found the tin of paint and the brush. In the tack-room cupboard, he found the tin. He emptied the sweets onto the bench.

He hadn't forgotten. The boy had made sure, teaching him slowly, going over and over it until he was certain that Mart May knew. If he had been afraid that he would not remember, the moment he held the full paintbrush over the tin, he knew that he was all right; he could see the letters, clear as lights in the sky. Slowly he began to copy them from the pictures in his head onto the tin.

M-A-R-T M-A-Y.

That night he slept without dreaming, without stirring.

After that he saw the letters everywhere, but now he was dissatisfied, hungry to learn the next, to piece all the black spikes together until they gave up their secrets.

22

Once or twice he bought a newspaper or a magazine and spent his lunch break picking out his own letters like individual thorns in a bramble bush. Once he saw his own name, M-A-Y, surrounded by other unknown marks, and seethed with frustration. He needed to know. He needed the boy.

He did not reappear until late the following spring. One afternoon, there were shouts from the far end of the garden; the next, the crunch of bicycle wheels on the gravel paths. Then, on his way from the beehives, he saw them – the boy, and another boy, shorter, darker. They were attaching an old apple crate to one of the bicycles with twine.

'You want wheels on that.'

They both looked up. Mart May saw the cloud-grey eyes with their skein of green for an instant, before the boy bent his head again.

The twine was tied and knotted. The box bumped and scraped along the gravel behind the bicycle, which they wheeled fast, up the path and out of sight, shouting.

The next day, Mart May listened out from early, but it was late in the afternoon before they came, crashing suddenly into the glade, pulling the bicycle and the apple box behind them. He had been about to open a hive.

'Hey, let's look, let's see the bees.'

'Not now you won't. Making all that racket. Drive 'em mad.'

'Oh.'

They turned away.

'I've something to show you,' Mart May said.

They paused, restless as the bees.

'What?'

'I've been waiting to show you all winter.'

They dropped the bicycle and followed him round to the tack room. He did not want both of them, was uncertain where he had felt proud.

'What is it?'

It was different, their talk, their restlessness. Everything was different.

He opened the wall cupboard and took out the tin. They watched, fidgeting. He looked at the boy, holding the tin up slightly.

'I thought,' Mart May shook up the tin violently, 'you'd like a mint.'

'Oh.'

He held the tin out with the painted letters towards them, not opening it, willing the boy to see, to notice, to know. To say.

But he only waited, shifting about, so that in the end the man simply took off the lid and offered the tin. Their hands dived and jostled inside, came up with sweets.

'Have two.'

'Hey, thanks.'

'Yes, thanks, Mart May.'

'Remembered my name then?'

'Oh yes.'

The man showed the tin again. 'Go on then,' he said.

'What?'

'See?'

'What?'

He turned it again and read, his finger following the letters, 'M-A-R-T M-A-Y. I painted that – "Mart May". After you'd gone away last year.'

A flicker passed over the boy's face. 'OK,' he said.

Mart May struggled, desperate not to have to ask, needing the boy to offer, to produce by some magic, the two books, the two pencils. Sweat prickled his neck. 'I could do with learning a bit more,' he said in the end. 'You teaching me again.'

The boy's face was the same, pale lashes, pale hair, white skin. But not the same.

The other one tugged at the apple box.

The boy glanced at Mart May and quickly away, as he turned after the apple box and the bicycle.

'You were right, Mart May,' he shouted, skidding away.

'What about?'

'You'll be bringing your pals here, you said. Plaguing. And now I have.'

The noise of them and the clattering box and the skidding gravel went on sounding through the glade. It took a long time for the quietness to return and while he waited for it Mart May stood quite still, turning the silver tin with the mints inside and the lettering on the outside, round and round slowly between his hands.

Father, Father

Father, Father

'I never realised,' Nita said, standing beside the washbasin rinsing out a tooth glass. Kay was turning a face flannel over and over between her hands, quite pointlessly.

'Dying. Do you mean about dying?'

'That. Yes.'

They were silent, contemplating it, the truth sinking in at last with the speaking of the word. In the room across the landing their mother was dying.

'I really meant Father.'

Naturally they had always seemed happy. Theirs had been the closest of families for thirty-seven years, Raymond and Elinor, Nita and Kay the two little girls. People used to point them out: 'The happy family.'

So they had taken it for granted that he loved her, as they loved her, fiercely and full of pride in her charm and her warmth and her skill, loved her more than they loved him, if they had ever had to choose.

Not that they did not love their father. But he was a man, and that itself set him outside their magic ring. They simply did not know him. Not as they knew one another, and knew her.

'But not this.'

Not this desperate, choking, terrified devotion, this anguish by her bed, this distraught clinging. This was a love they could not recognise and did not know how to deal with – and even, in a way, resented. And so they fussed over him, his refusal to eat, his red eyes, the flesh withering on his frame; they took him endless cups of tea, coffee, hot water with lemon, but otherwise could not face his anguished, embarrassing love, and the fear on his face, his openness to grief.

The end was agony, though perhaps it was more so for them, for their mother seemed unaware of it all now. She had slipped down out of reach.

It lasted for hours. There was a false alarm. The doctor came. Next she rallied, and even seemed about to wake briefly, before drowning again.

They had both gone to sleep, Nita on the sewing-room sofa under a quilt, Kay in the kitchen rocking chair, slumped awkwardly across her arm. But some change woke them and they both went into the hall, looking at one another in terror, scarcely believing, icy calm. They went up the stairs without speaking.

Afterwards, and for the rest of their lives, the picture was branded on their minds and the branding marks became deeper and darker and more ineradicable with everything that happened. So that what might have been a tender, fading memory became a bitter scar. Their father was kneeling beside the bed. He had her hand between both of his and clutched to his breast, and his tears were splashing down onto it and running over it. Every few minutes a groan came from him, a harsh, raw sound which appalled them.

The lamp was on, tipped away from her face and the golden-yellow curtains she had chosen for their cheerful brightness during the day were now dull topaz. The bedside table was a litter of bottles and pots of medicines.

Her breathing was hoarse, as if her chest was a gravel bed through which water was trying to strain. Now and then it heaved up and collapsed down again. But the rest of her body was almost flat to the bed, almost a part of it. She was so thin, the bedclothes were scarcely lifted.

Nita felt for Kay's hand and pressed until it hurt,

though neither of them was aware of it. Their father was still bent over the figure on the bed, still holding, holding on.

And then, shocking them, everything stopped. There was a rasping breath, and after it, nothing, simply nothing at all, and the world stopped turning and waited, though what was being waited for they could not have told.

That split second fell like a drop of balm in the tumult of her dying and their distress, so that long afterwards each of them would try to recall it for comfort. But almost at once it was driven out by the cataract of grief and rage that poured from their father. The bellow of pain that horrified them so that in the end they fled down to the sitting room, and held each other and wept, but quietly, and with a restraint and dignity that was shared and unspoken.

There was to be a funeral tea, though not many would come. She had outlived most of her relatives and had needed few friends, their family unit had been so tight, yielding her all she had wanted.

But those who did come must be properly entertained.

Nita and Kay arrived back before the rest to prepare, though the work had been done by Mrs Willis and her daughter.

The hall was cool. Nita, standing in front of the mirror to take off her hat and tidy her hair, caught her sister's eye. They were exhausted. The whole day, like the whole week, seemed unreal, something they had floated through. Their father had wept uncontrollably in the church, and at the graveside bent forward so far, as the coffin was lowered, that they had half-feared he was about to pitch himself in after it.

Behind Nita, Kay's face was pinched, the eye sockets bruise-coloured. There was everything to say. There was nothing to say. The clock ticked.

She will never hear it tick again, Nita thought.

For a second, then, the truth found an entrance and a response, but there was no time, the cars had returned, there were footsteps on the path, voices. The truth retreated again.

They turned, faces composed. Nita opened the door.

Every day for the next six months they thought that he would die too. If he did not, it was not any will to live that prevented it. He scarcely ate. He saw no one. He scarcely spoke. He had always been interested in money, money was his work, his hobby, his passion. Now, the newspapers lay unopened, bank letters and packets of company reports gathered dust. For much of the time he sat in the drawing room opposite his wife's chair. Often he wept. Whenever he could persuade Nita or Kay to sit with him he talked about their mother. Within the half-year she had achieved sainthood and become perfect in the memory, every detail about her sacred, every aspect of their marriage without flaw.

'I miss her,' Kay said, one evening in October. They were in the kitchen, tidying round, putting away, laying the table for breakfast.

Nita sat down abruptly. The kitchen went silent. It had been said. Somehow, until now, they had not dared.

'Yes.'

'I miss laughing with her over the old photographs, I miss watching her embroider. Her hands.'

'People don't now, do they? There used to be all those little shops for silks and threads and transfers.'

They thought of her sewing box, in the drawing

room by the French windows, and the last, intricate piece, unfinished on the round wood frame.

'Things will never be the same, Kay.'

'But they will get better. Surely they'll get better.'

'I suppose so.'

'Perhaps – we ought at least to start looking at some of the things.'

The sewing box, her desk, the drawers and wardrobe in her bedroom. Clothes, earrings, hairbrushes, letters, embroidery silks were spread out for inspection in their minds.

'You read about people quarrelling with their mothers.'

'We never quarrelled.'

'You couldn't.'

'You read about it being the natural way of things.'

'Quarrelling is not obligatory.'

They caught one another's eye and Nita laughed. The laughter grew, and took them gradually over; they laughed until they cried, and sat back exhausted, muscles aching, and the laughter broke something, some seal that had been put on life to keep it down.

Outside Nita's room, they held one another, knowing that the laughter had marked a change.

In the study, hearing their laughter coming faintly from the distant kitchen, their father let misery and loneliness and self-pity wash over him, and sank back, submerging himself under the wave.

What would life be like? They did not know. Each morning they went out of the house together, at the same time, and parted at the end of the next street. Nita walked on, to her hospital reception desk. Kay caught her bus to the department store where she was Ladies' Fitter.

At six they met again, and walked home. And so, life was the same, it went on in the old way – yet it did not. Even the shape of the trees in the avenue seemed changed. When they neared the house something came over them, some miasma of sorrow and fear and uncertainty, and a sort of dread.

Each knew that the other felt it, but neither spoke of it; they spoke, as before, of the ordinary details of the day, the weather, the news of the town.

And in each of their minds was always the question – will today be different? Will this be the day when he wakes from the terrible paralysis of misery?

But when the door opened into the cool, silent hall

and the light caught the bevel of the mirror, they knew at once that after all, this was not the day, and went in to hang their coats and empty this or that bag, to wash and tidy before going in to him.

The medicines had been thrown away and a few bills and receipts and shopping lists, otherwise he would allow nothing to be sorted or moved or cleared.

Everything must remain as she had left it.

Once, a few days after the funeral, Kay had crept into her mother's bedroom and sat on the bed, which the nurse had stripped and re-made with fresh linen, as if, somehow, her mother might come back and it must be ready for her. And she had been everywhere in the room. Kay had touched the dressing gown behind the door, and the touch had disturbed the faint fine smell of the violet talcum powder and soap her mother had used, and brought her back even more vividly.

Six months later, nothing had been moved, but going into the room again, in search of her mother's old address book, she had sensed the difference at once. There was a hollow, she was no longer there. The bedroom was quite empty of her.

Kay had found, as she stood for a few moments at the window looking out over the garden, that she could not conjure her mother up in any way, could not picture her, could not remember the sound of her voice. When she touched the dressing gown, the smell had gone.

'Father ought to go in there now,' she said, going in to Nita. 'Surely it might . . .'

Her sister shook her head.

'Perhaps Dr Boyle —'

'But he isn't ill.'

'I suppose not.'

'Perhaps you are right though, about the room.'

'What should we say?'

They imagined what words might conceivably serve, where they might possibly begin.

'It would be best to be straightforward,' Nita said at last.

'Could you?'

'I — I think I must.'

But two days later, it was Kay who spoke, coming into the drawing room and finding it in darkness, so that she startled him by clicking on the light.

There had been some petty irritations during the day and she was suffering from a cold; if it had not been for those things she might never have confronted him, would never have had the courage.

'Whatever are you doing sitting here in the dark again, Father? Whatever good is this going to do any of us?'

She saw that she had shocked him and his shock gave her nerve.

'It is six months since Mother died, half a year. What good are you doing? We have to go out, carry on a life. That's how it should be, how it has to be. Do you think we haven't felt it and missed her as much as you? Do you suppose she would think well of you, hiding away, wringing your hands? You've interest in nothing, concern for nothing. You're in the half-dark. Have you wondered how it is for us, coming back to it at the end of every day?'

She heard herself as she might hear someone in a play. She was not startled or made afraid by her own voice, or the passion with which she had spoken. She simply heard herself, with interest but without emotion and when she stopped speaking, she heard the silence.

Her father was staring at her, his face brick-red, his mouth working.

She began to shake.

It was Nita who saved them, coming without any warning into the room.

'Kay?'

She looked at her sister, at her father, at the two shocked faces and though she had heard nothing of what had been said, the force of it seemed to press down upon the silence that filled the room and Nita understood the enormity of what had happened.

'Kay?'

But Kay was frozen, she could neither speak nor move, could scarcely even breathe.

And then he got up and without looking at either of them, blundered out of the room, and through the hall towards the stairs.

When they returned home the following evening he was not in the house. He had left before ten, Mrs Willis said, in a taxi which was taking him in to the city.

By the time he returned they had gone to bed, though both were lying awake, turning the events over in their minds. Both heard his key in the lock, his footsteps, the closing of his bedroom door. Both thought of creeping along the corridor to the other. Neither did.

The next day, the pattern was the same, and so, until the end of that week, on the Saturday, he ate lunch and supper with them. But something in his look forbade them to refer to any of it. Kay was terrified of catching his eye.

'He is my father, why should I be afraid of him?'

The news was on the television, the one programme they always watched, as they had watched it every night with their mother. Somehow, speaking over the voices on it seemed to Kay like not quite speaking at all.

The news ended. Nita got up.

'He should be grateful to us,' she said and her voice rose. 'Grateful!'

Her sister's face had flushed and Kay saw that there were tears in her eyes.

'It had to stop and I didn't have the courage to say it.'

She went quickly out of the room. Kay stared at

the blank screen, and quite suddenly, her mother's face came to mind; she saw her as she had been, long before the illness, saw her grey, neatly parted hair and the soft cheeks, saw her smiling, pleased, patient expression. She had gone and now she had come back.

The television screen remained opaque and grey.

'Yes,' Kay said to herself. 'Yes.'

As she left the sewing room where they kept the television set her father came out of his study and instinctively Kay stepped back, acutely conscious of what had been said earlier.

'Kay.'

She found herself reaching out, and then held by him, her face against his sleeve, pressed into the cloth, smelling his soap and the faint smell of his city day which brought her childhood back to envelop her and hold her as he held her himself.

Nothing else was said after the one word 'Kay' and in a second or two he disengaged himself gently and went down the passage towards the side door that led to the garden. Every night, until the last weeks of her mother's life, he had gone there at the end of the evening to smoke a single small cigar. Kay went up to her bedroom and opened the window and after a moment the smell of the smoke came to her from the garden below.

She felt a rush of the most exhilarating happiness, as the anxiety and gloom of the past weeks fell away. The house had been sunk into the dreary aftermath of their mother's death for so long that she had forgotten even the small, pleasant details of everyday life until now, when one of them had been given back. They were all weary, their flesh felt dead, their skins grey, their movements were slow; there had been no lightness in anything, the subdued atmosphere had become usual, their father's isolated uncommunicated grief suffocating everything that might have been enjoyed or anticipated.

She leaned further out of the window, intent on catching as much as possible of the smell of his cigar smoke.

We have come through it, she thought. We have come through.

She was not rash enough to expect life to be everything that it had been. Their mother was dead.

Nothing could alter that, nothing lessened the pain though the death had been 'a blessing'.

But something had changed at last. They had all moved on and surely for good.

She waited at the open window until the last trace of smoke had faded from the air and the only smell was of night, and grass and the earth. Then she got into bed, and slept like something new born.

And indeed, slowly, gradually the mood in the house lightened. Their father spoke to them, went out, returned with the evening paper, opened letters, worked at his desk. There was no laughter yet, and no social life. Friends and neighbours were not invited. But they had all of them lost the habit of that and did not feel any particular need yet to re-acquire it.

'In the summer,' Nita said.

'Perhaps we could have one of the old summer garden parties.'

'I wonder – do you think Father has given any thought to a holiday?'

Such small exchanges lightened their days. There was no sense of urgency or anxiety, no need to push forward too fast. But when they spoke of their mother now it was with smiling reminiscence, only tinged at the edges with sorrow.

On a Wednesday evening, almost eight months after the death, they walked down the avenue together as usual, and into the house.

'Hello?'

Sometimes they returned first, sometimes he did, and so one or other always called out.

'Hello?'

It was late spring but exceptionally warm. The drawing-room door was open. Nita went through.

The French windows were also open. From the garden came voices speaking quietly together.

'Kay.'

'What's wrong?'

'There is — there's someone in the garden with Father.'

They looked at one another, recognising the next step taken, the next stage reached.

'Good,' Kay said. 'Isn't that good?'

Though they had to wait and absorb it, take in the feeling of strangeness. No one else had been in the house since the day of the funeral. Now someone was here, some old friend of his, some neighbour, and although if asked they would each have said that they welcomed it, nevertheless it felt like a violation of something that had grown to become sacred.

The clock ticked in the hall behind them.

'Oh goodness,' Kay said, half-laughing with impatience at their own hesitation, and walked boldly out through the open windows onto the terrace.

The scene, and the next moments that passed, took their place in the series of ineradicable pictures etched into their minds, joining their mother's deathbed, the funeral, the sight of their father leaning over the grave.

Two garden chairs were drawn up on either side of the small table. Two cups and saucers, the teapot, milk jug and sugar bowl stood on the table. That fact alone they had difficulty in absorbing, and wondered wildly how the tea had come to be made and found its way out there.

Hearing them, their father turned, but did not get up.

Kay and Nita hesitated like children uncertain of what to say or do next, needing permission to come forward. They were on the outside of a charmed circle.

'Here you are!' he said.

After another moment, and as one, they began to cross the grass.

'This is a friend of mine — Leila. Leila Crocker.' He gestured expansively. 'My daughters. Nita. Kay.'

They knew, Nita said afterwards. They knew absolutely and at once and their stomachs plunged like lifts down a deep shaft, leaving only nausea.

The garden froze, the colours were blanched out of everything, the leaves stiffened, the trees went dead. Unbelievably, instinctively, impossibly, they knew.

She stood. Said, 'How very nice.'

Under their feet, deep below the grass and turf, the earth seemed to shift and heave treacherously, shaking their confidence, throwing them off balance. The sky tipped and ended up on its side, like a house after a bomb had fallen.

At the moment of death, it is said, a person's past rushes towards them, but it was the whole of the future that they saw, in the instant between taking in the presence of the woman with their father, and her words; and in composing themselves to greet her, they saw what was to come in every aspect and detail, it seemed.

'But that cannot have been so,' Nita said, years later. Yet it had. They knew that absolutely.

But all they saw was a woman, of perhaps forty-five, perhaps a few years less or a few years more, who wore a cherry-red suit and had hair formed in an extraordinary bolster above her brow, and who was called Leila Crocker.

'Leila,' she said quickly; 'please call me that.'

They would not. At once they retreated into themselves like snails touched on the tenderest tips of their horns. They could not possibly call her Leila, and so they called her nothing at all.

'I'm afraid the tea will have gone cold.' And she touched the china pot with the blue ribbon pattern. Nita and Kay flinched, though giving no outward sign. The last woman to have touched the blue ribbon teapot had been their mother.

'Not that we've left much of it I'm afraid.'

Their father's voice sounded quite different to them. Lighter, younger, the tone oddly jovial. Everything about him was lighter and younger. He sat back smiling, leaning back in the garden chair, looking at the blue ribbon teapot, and at the woman.

'No please.' Nita made a strange little gesture, like a half-bow. 'Don't worry. We always make tea freshly.'

No one moved then. No one else spoke.

We make a tableau, Kay thought, or one of those old pictures. 'Tea in the Garden' – no, 'A Visitor to Tea'.

Their father might have spoken then, might have told them to take their freshly made tea into the garden to join them. The woman might have said, observing their evening routine, that she must go. But he did not, she did not; they sat, as if waiting to resume an interrupted conversation, so that in the end it was Nita who broke the tableau, by turning and going quickly back across the lawn and through the open French window into the house. Kay gave a half-smile, as if in some kind of hopeless explanation or apology – though meaning neither – before following her sister. Just at the window, she glanced quickly back, expecting them to be watching, feeling their eyes on her. But her father and the woman were turned towards one another, both leaning forwards slightly, their eager conversation eagerly resumed.

We might not have been here, Kay thought.

In the kitchen, Nita dropped the lid of the kettle and the sound went on reverberating on the tiled floor, even after she had bent impatiently to pick it up.

Rain poured off the roofs of the houses they walked past and the early blossom lay in sad, sodden little heaps in the gutter. Spring had retreated behind banked, swollen clouds and a cold wind.

'Perhaps it is time for us to leave home,' Kay said into the umbrella with which she was trying to shield her head and face. Nita stopped dead and lifted her own umbrella to stare at her sister and the rain flowed off it down her neck.

'Even without . . . well, there will surely be changes. Perhaps we should institute our own.'

'Why must there be changes?'

'Aren't we rather too old to be living at home still?'

Kay was thirty-five, Nita about thirty-seven. They looked older. Felt older.

'But wherever would we go to? Where would you want to go?'

'A flat?'

'Do you like flats?'

'Not particularly.'

'We are perfectly happy and comfortable as we are.'

'Yes.'

They turned the corner. Each had had a private inner glimpse into the rooms of a small flat, and looked quickly away.

'Besides.'

The rest was unspoken, and perfectly understood. Besides, Nita would have continued, now that she has come to the house there is all the more reason than ever for us to stay.

Every afternoon since that first day when they had stepped into the garden and seen their father sitting with Leila Crocker over the blue ribbon teapot, they had dreaded coming home and finding her there again. Twice already they had done so. Once, the two of them had been seated in exactly the same place in the garden, the table and the tea things between them so that they might never have moved at all.

The next time, Leila Crocker had been coming along the passage from the downstairs cloakroom as they opened the front door. None of them had known what to say.

Now, Kay turned her key in the lock, pushed the door slowly and waited. They both waited, listening. But the house was empty, they could feel at once. It felt and sounded and smelled empty. The clock ticked. Nita took both umbrellas out to the scullery.

At the end of the television news, when Kay had switched off the set, their father had not come home.

'He has never said anything.'

'Perhaps he has nothing to say.'

'He has told us nothing about her. Wouldn't it be usual – to tell something?'

'What is "usual"? I don't think I know.'

'No.'

It was not that he had behaved secretively, or evasively, or avoided them. Things had gone on exactly as before. Except that in some vital, deep-rooted way, they had not. Because always, no matter how he behaved, the woman was between the three of them.

The taxi came for him each morning. He went out, returned, sometimes very late, opened his letters, read the newspaper, worked at his desk, smoked his single late cigar. When they were all together, he ate with them. When he was not at home, they had no idea of where he was and could not ask.

The house seemed suddenly imbued with meaning, redolent of their past and precious to them. Every door handle and window-pane and cupboard. Every book and curtain and step on the stairs. The mirror in the hall and the clock and the blue ribbon teapot, all seemed to hold the life of their family within every atom, to be infinitely more than household objects made of wood and glass and metal and china and paint. Every touch and footstep, the echo of every word spoken, was part of the fabric and substance of the house. At night they lay and wrapped it round themselves and held it to them.

They were possessive, passionate and jealous of it and everything it contained. The feeling they had for it was as strong and vital as their love for their father and the memory of their mother. They were shocked by the power of it.

They could not say that they liked Leila Crocker. They could not say that they disliked her.

'Her hair is very tightly permed,' Kay said.

'But her shoes are good.'

At the department store during one lunch hour Kay had suddenly told the other fitter about it. Anne McKay's hirsute face had lit up.

'Oh, Kay, that is so very nice! Isn't that nice for him? I think that's lovely.'

What is 'lovely'? Kay thought, panicking. I have told her that he brought a woman to tea. Her face betrayed her terror. Anne McKay reached out and touched her arm. They were seated in the old broken-down basket chairs in the dusty little staffroom.

'I meant how lovely for him to have some companionship. I know you miss your mother, of course you do, but life has to move on.'

Does it? Why does it? Why can it not stay as it is? Kay took a bite from her sandwich but could not swallow it.

'You won't be at home for ever, will you? Either of you.'

Won't we? Why not? Why should we ever leave? Who could make us?

Kay jumped up, and went to the cloakroom and there spat the piece of sandwich violently into the lavatory basin.

'I suppose,' Nita said, hearing about it later, 'that companionship is important.'

'He has us. He isn't alone.'

'We should try to be fair.'

'What is "unfair"?'

'We are — well, isn't it quite different?'

'From what?'

'I mean, it is just a different kind of companionship — friendship. Of course it is, Kay.'

But what the nature of the friendship or companionship was they could not have said.

It had been raining for almost a week, but now, as they walked the last hundred yards down the avenue, the sun came out and shone in their faces and reflected watery gold on the wet pavement and the house roof.

'We must try to be fair,' Nita said again.

They quickened their steps.

But the house was empty, as it was empty every evening for the next week, and after that, it seemed, was never empty again. It was the speed of it all that horrified them, the speed which was, Kay said, unnecessary and unseemly.

'And rather hurtful.'

But their father was now oblivious to everything except the woman he was to marry. For he would marry Leila Crocker, he said, telling them, with neither warning nor ceremony, the next time he spent an evening at home with them.

'I should like you to know,' he had said, laying down his soup spoon, 'that I have asked Leila to be my wife.'

The room went deathly silent and, it seemed to Kay and Nita, deathly cold. A chill mist seemed to creep in under the door and the window frame, curling itself round them so that they actually shivered. They could not look at him or at one another. They could do nothing.

'I have found a very dear companion, a very fine person with whom to share the rest of my life. Your mother – her illness and her death – were – very difficult. I had not imagined – of course you hardly know Leila, but you will come to know her, and to love and admire her, I am quite certain of it. Quite certain.'

He beamed innocently from one to the other.

'This is going to be a very happy home once more.'

*

It was like their bereavement all over again but in a way worse, because death was the final certainty, and this was uncertain, this would go on and on. Their whole lives would change but they did not know how. Their future would be entirely different but they could not picture it.

That first night, after he had told them, the silence had been so terrible, his eager, beaming face so open and expectant, that Nita had prayed to die, then, there, rather than have to face any of it and Kay had wished her tongue cut out, for any words she might feel able to utter would be wrong and false and surely choke her.

In the end, after what might have been a minute or a lifetime, their father said, 'I hope very much that you are pleased.'

Kay swallowed.

'Of course, your mother —'

Nita leaped up, pushing her chair back with such force that it toppled and crashed over behind her. 'She — Mother has nothing to do with this — please do not talk about Mother.'

'Perhaps —' Kay heard her own voice, strangled

and peculiar. 'Perhaps you may be able to understand what a shock this is.'

'But you *are* happy for me? You do share this happiness with me?'

His face was that of a child anxious for approval, and their feelings as they looked at him were impossible, confused, painful.

'She has given me a new life.'

They fled.

The next morning Nita woke Kay up before seven o'clock.

'I am going to the service. Will you come?'

Kay turned onto her back. They had not been to church since the Sunday after the funeral.

'What will you pray for?'

'Guidance.'

'For him?'

'For ourselves.'

'For it to end – for this – this thing to be over.'

Nita sat down on her sister's bed. 'I think,' she said carefully, 'that it will not.'

'No.'

'And I find I cannot cope with – I have never felt like this in my life.'

'What do you feel?'

'I think it is hatred. And anger. Great anger.'

'Betrayal.'

'Is it?'

'But not us – it is not us he is betraying.'

'No.'

'It is indecent. He is an old man.'

'Perhaps if it had been in a few years' time.'

'That is the worst, isn't it? Think of all those tears. All that – and now to think it was all lies and falseness.'

'Oh I don't think it was. He did –'

'Love Mother?'

'Yes.'

'Then how could he?'

'If I don't deal with this terrible hatred it will become destructive of everything. I hardly slept.'

'Burrowing.'

'Yes. It's like that. A canker. Will you come?'

'No.'

'We have to try. We must try.'

'For her sake?'

59

'No, for him. Of course for him.'

'Do you like her?'

'We barely know her. I only say we should try.'

'You are too good.'

Kay turned over and pressed her face hard into her pillow. Her mother seemed to be somewhere in the depths of it, as she was everywhere now, smiling, patient. Betrayed. 'You will have to go by yourself,' Kay said, tears pouring down her face.

The city restaurant had been full at ten minutes past one and so they had been obliged to share a table. That was how they had met.

'I suppose she had been on the lookout for just such a man, eating alone.'

'Kay —'

'Unfair?'

'Yes.'

'It is all unfair.'

'She is very nice to us.'

'Why should she not be?'

'We have not been altogether nice to her — we have perhaps been rather unwelcoming.'

'Of course we have. She is unwelcome.'

Though so far Leila Crocker had behaved impeccably. She had been reserved, friendly but never effusive. Pleasant and careful.

'It really is difficult to dislike her,' Nita said.

'I don't care for her clothes.'

'Well they are perfectly good clothes.'

'Oh yes. *Good* clothes.'

Leila Crocker wore smart suits in plain colours, alternating them week by week, cherry-red, ice-blue, camel, mauve. She was, she said, personal assistant to a managing director. The second time she came to the house, she told them that she was forty-four.

'Why did she suppose her age was of any interest to us? It is no business of ours.'

Their father was almost thirty years older. They could not talk to him.

'I hope that things will go on as they always have,' he said.

'How can they? How can anything ever be as it was?'

Kay ran her finger over and over the closed lid of the piano.

'He is destroying all of it.'

'Do stop doing that.'

'Do you suppose he ever thinks – thinks of Mother?'

'Surely he must.'

'What? What can he think?'

'You will take off the veneer.'

'There is no one else left to defend her memory.'

'Is that what we are for?'

'What else?'

'It is almost as though thirty-seven years had somehow –'

'Well they have not.' Kay spoke in a raw, furious whisper.

'Do stop doing that. I think I shall go mad,' Nita shouted, then went quite silent. They stared at one another fearfully.

'Look,' Kay said after a moment. 'Look what is happening, what it is making us do. Everything is cracking and splintering and being destroyed. Even us.'

A month after Leila Crocker had first come to the house, Nita found her in the kitchen one evening.

'I am cooking for us all.'

'Oh, there is no need. I was going to make omelettes with a salad.'

'I'm sure you would prefer roast chicken.'

'And then,' Nita said, going in, trembling, to her sister's room, 'I noticed it.'

'Noticed what?'

'How can he think of doing such a thing? How can he?'

The light had caught the ring on Leila Crocker's hand as she had reached out to one of the kitchen taps.

Kay laid down her pen. Her diary was open on the desk in front of her.

'The diamond hoop with the small sapphires?'

'Yes.'

Though their mother had rarely worn it, saying it was too special, too dressy, it was to be kept for very special occasions, and those had rarely come, in such quiet, self-contained lives.

'Are you sure?'

The words came out of Kay's mouth as heavy and cold and separate as marbles.

'Go down and see for yourself. If he has to give her a ring – well, people naturally do –'

'Not the ring that belonged to their wife of thirty-seven years who has been dead for under a year. I think not.'

At two o'clock in the morning, Kay went into her sister's room and, after hesitating a moment, her bed.

'Ninny?' She had not used the name for twenty years.

'I'm not asleep.'

'I don't think I can bear it.'

'I know.'

'I feel as if I were a child.'

'What would other people do? Different kinds of people?'

Kay thought of Anne McKay, and Mrs Willis. 'Do you – do you believe she can know?'

They lay, picturing their mother, floating somewhere nearby, smiling, patient.

Is it for her? Nita thought, feeling her sister's warmth to the side of her. As children they had often crept into one another's beds. Is it really for Mother's sake that I mind what is happening more than I have ever minded anything apart from her dying?

But in the end she turned on her side and took her

sister's hand and, after a few moments, slept, exhausted by the impossible, unanswerable questions.

'We cannot possibly go to the wedding,' Kay had said. But of course they did, and somehow got through the service, at which there were three hymns and two readings and Leila Crocker wore cream lace. The church and the hotel room afterwards were full of strangers. Their father's face was flushed with excitement and open devotion.

Somehow, they got through all of it. Somehow, they stayed until the car had left the hotel courtyard, waved at by the strangers.

In the avenue, Kay stopped, took off her jacket and shook it out until the few paper rose petals drifted into the gutter.

The two weeks that followed were extraordinarily happy. They felt an unreal sense of freedom and contentment, in the house by themselves, answerable to no one. The sun shone; they set the table up on the terrace and ate supper there, and, at the weekend, breakfast and lunch as well.

They put a shield around themselves. Neither

referred to their father or to the marriage. When postcards arrived, first from Rome, and then from Florence, they read and then discarded them without a word.

But on the morning they were due to return Nita cut fresh branches of philadelphus and put them in jugs about the house.

'We have to try. We have a duty to try. Things may go perfectly well.'

From the very beginning they did not, though whose fault it was none of them could have told.

It was difficult to share their home with another, difficult to accept her as having precedence over them, difficult that she and their father slept in the same room, the old room in which their mother had slept in the years before her last illness, difficult to get used to changes of daily routine and the presence of their stepmother's possessions hanging in wardrobes, filling drawers, displacing the old order of things. Difficult to find someone else in the house every evening when they returned home, at supper, at breakfast and for the whole of every weekend.

'Difficult, difficult, difficult,' Kay said, walking faster than usual up the avenue.

But difficult might have become less so. They might perhaps have adapted themselves to the new arrangement, in the end. Difficult was not painful or hurtful and it was pain and hurt which came very quickly.

'What is happening?' Nita said as they rounded the corner, and saw the removal van outside the house. 'What is happening?'

They almost ran.

It was nearly over. The work had been going on for most of the day. All the old furniture from their mother's sewing room and the small sitting room, as well as from the bedroom in which she had died, had gone. In the sitting room were a new, bright-blue sofa and chair, and a glass-fronted cabinet. The sewing room and bedroom were empty.

Their father met them in the hall, saw their faces, but could not manage to meet their eyes.

After that everything disintegrated, everything was swept away, or so it felt. Their mother's clothes were cleared, and her papers. The photographs of her about the drawing room and their father's study disappeared, though her pearls and her two pairs of good earrings did not go, their stepmother wore them.

'How dare she?' Kay said, banging into her father's study. 'How dare she take Mother's things, her personal things, how could you let her?'

'Please lower your voice. I remember that when your mother passed away —'

'Died. She died.'

'— you — and Nita — you said you would prefer not to have those things. As I understood.'

'That did not give — your wife — the right to appropriate them.'

He stood up. 'I gave them to her. I wanted her to have them. Leila took nothing.'

'How could you give them — you?'

'I think, I believe, that it is what —'

'If you say it is what Mother would have wanted, I think I shall kill you.'

'Kay —'

'You let her throw out our mother's furniture — clear her things.'

'We did it together. It was time.'

'For who?'

'For me.'

'You are a blind, cruel, besotted, foolish old man.'

At the top of the stairs, she almost collided heavily with Nita.

'Whatever is happening? Why were you screaming?'

In her own room, Kay sobbed tears of bitter pain and rage.

Nita had closed the door. 'It is very hard,' she said. 'I hate this. I mind it as much as you do. I mind it for Mother's sake and for us, but screaming at Father is not right – he loves her, he is besotted with her. He cannot see that she is doing anything wrong.'

'He is being treacherous, utterly treacherous. He was married to Mother for almost forty years. He loved her, he saw her die and almost went mad with grief. We had to watch all that, bear all that. He has utterly, utterly betrayed her, bringing that woman here, marrying her in such haste, such a few months after – and making that – that vulgar display, that wedding – giving her Mother's jewellery, helping her throw Mother's things away – taking down the photographs.

'She has no idea, none. She is completely insensitive and I do not care for her, I wish she had never come here — but I don't blame her and I do not hate her. I blame him. I hate him. I can't forgive him — I cannot —'

The tears this time were not of anger, but of misery and grief at everything lost, and after a moment Nita cried with her for the same loss, of their mother and of everything that had been hers, and for the loss of him, the loss of all love, for it seemed that their father had taken everything from them, and given it to his wife, taken his love for them and for their mother and theirs for him, taken his loyalty and sense of what was right. Taken their home and their place in it.

They sat holding one another on Kay's bed as the light faded, and the empty room below and the empty room next door were like hollow caves carved out of their own hearts.

They lived in the house for another five months, and in that time everything changed, piece by piece. Everything that was old and familiar and belonged to their past went and was replaced by the new, the strange, until only their father's study and their own rooms remained unaltered. They scarcely spoke to him, avoided him altogether if they could. To their stepmother they were polite, with all the careful, wary courtesy of strangers, but they saw, in her face, in her eyes, that she was indifferent to them.

'They neither need nor want us,' Nita said, 'that much is clear without anything being said.'

They felt invisible, quite supplanted, quite irrelevant. One evening they drew a circle on the street map, and began to look within it. They could not have borne to change their routine, the walk to the same bus stop, the return together. It was all that was left to them, apart from their jobs, and their own shared life.

When they found a flat which would do, Kay told their father, who said nothing. 'You have your own lives to lead,' their stepmother said brightly; 'naturally you do.'

The flat was really quite pleasant. The sitting room had wide windows overlooking the chestnut trees that lined the quiet street. The rooms were freshly painted. They grew used to not having a garden, particularly as it was winter when they moved in.

They wondered from time to time whether they had judged Leila Crocker, as they still thought of her, correctly, whether she had cornered their father into a meeting, marriage, the clearing away of his past, or whether she had in fact been blameless and the fault was his, but it came to matter less and less just as, to their surprise, they were able to remember their mother more clearly in the flat than they had in the old house. She had come with them, she was there every evening on their return, in her photograph, which was everywhere, and with her invisible yet smiling, patient presence.

They thought as little as possible about their father and their old home, though it was the memories of home which gave them the greatest pain, striking without warning, because of the way the sun shone suddenly through a window, or the banging of a gate. At these moments, the past would wash over them and drown them in itself. Their years of childhood and young womanhood were fresher and more vivid than the previous day so that it seemed they might simply have opened the door and walked back into them.

Their habits firmed, hardened, their natures set.

Routine became all-important. They came to dread any disturbance, any hint of the unfamiliar.

Their father's new marriage had nothing to do with them.

'It is far better,' Kay said; 'it is the only way.' And all the while believed it.

But very occasionally, Nita got up before her and went to the early service. Kay could never be persuaded. It was the only rift between them, and slight enough, apart from the day Nita let the blue ribbon teapot slip out of her hands onto the floor of the kitchenette, where it smashed into far too many pieces for there to be the slightest hope of repair. Walking into the room a moment later, Kay found her sister standing, staring down at the shards of china and, recognising them, she began to scream, furiously, uncontrollably, her voice rising and rising, until Nita's face took on a look of pain, and panic, and, as Kay's scream intensified, of fear.

Need
———

Need

One of the Morris kids had let Rosa's hen out and was chasing the poor flapping thing round, both of them squawking together and mud flying.

That's all the site was that year, mud. We were in it for a month and I think it rained every day. At night I lay in the bunk and went to sleep to it, slamming on the van roof and rolling down the sides.

'Get off. Get away.' I couldn't catch him of course. He ducked and dived off. All the Morris kids are quicksilver, it's in them to be. But I got the hen without much trouble. She just cowered in the mud and let me pick her up and, when I held her funny, soft, wet body between my hands, went very still.

Then it came.

'Hooey – oo. Hooey – oo.'

I froze like the hen, waiting.

'Hooey – Ssssss . . .'

I couldn't see him and in any case he was clever at

throwing his voice. I held onto the hen tighter for comfort.

'Hooey – oo.' No one else would have heard it. He whistle-whispered in a queer, sing-song way. It made my neck prickle.

I hated him. Little Midge, the whistler, somewhere here, pressed up against one of the vans, or in the dark slit between two of them, or skulking behind a tent flap.

Rosa's hen jerked its head round suddenly and I saw its unblinking little eye, round as a button. Something in the gleam of it gave me nerve and I walked wildly round the back of Rosa's van, opened the door of the cage slung below it and bundled the hen in. Rain dripped from the overhead awning down my back.

From somewhere close by a baby set up a wail and that started another, and set the ponies off one by one, geeing and braying and whinnying.

I found that one of the worst things. That it was never quiet. I'd been born into it and grown up with it and never accepted it. There's always a racket, day and night, children, animals, musicians, all jammed together, living and breathing and playing and fighting in one place. I used to walk away sometimes, along the cliff path and down onto the secret beach, just to get away from it. To get some quiet. The sea was never quiet, but that was different. The sea was a peaceful noise.

Otherwise, and when we were in other places where escape was not so easy, I had to make do with going to Rosa. I did that now, once I'd stuffed the bird back in its cage.

The van was dark, as it always was. The only light came when you opened the door curtain to climb in and a slant of it cut through the felty oil-filled blackness.

She had the lamp on, a painted metal one that stood behind her back, and another hanging from a hook in the ceiling. There was one on her fortune-telling table too, but that was only lit when she was working.

If I close my eyes I can smell the smell inside that van, the oil and the sweet heavy smell from the little pots of dried stuff Rosa burned, and Rosa's sweat. She wasn't exactly dirty but she didn't change her black clothes often either. I can feel the thick darkness like wool on my skin. I didn't need a light in there any more than Rosa did, I knew my way by feel. There was no spare space. Hers was one of the last of the old vans, the barrel sort with steps up the painted sides. Everyone else had modern vans.

Rosa was lying on her back and she had her wig off. I could see it hanging up with the black veil and its gold coins attached.

'One of the Morris kids had let the hen out,' I said. 'I've put her back now.'

I sat down on the stool under the cabinet. The glass and china caught the light from the oil lamps here and there.

Rosa's cabinet was her pride.

'I'm not well, Biddy.' And her voice sounded odd. I could see her now my eyes had got used to the half-dark. She was curled up facing me. The knitted blanket pulled round her neck. Her bald head shone like the china plates.

'What's wrong? I'd better fetch Ma.'

'Your Ma can't do anything.'

'Was it something you ate?'

'No.'

'Shall I make you a cup of tea then?'

We always had tea. Partly for itself, and then for

Rosa to tell my future in the leaves. I think she practised on me.

She'd tell me what sort of day I'd had, whichever school I happened to be going to at the time. It wasn't easy, changing schools every few weeks, leaving one, starting another, then going back all over again. Rosa would make the tea leaves reassuring to help me.

But she didn't want any tea, she said.

'Just sit quiet with me, Biddy.'

Well, I was happy with that and we stayed quiet for a long time. The rain dripped on the roof and now and then someone called out but it seemed far away and the ponies had settled down again. Once I refrayed the wick and pumped the lever to make the oil lamp flare.

Rosa's breathing sounded harsh as shaken nails.

I said, 'Little Midge was out here. Before.'

She was the only one I'd been able to tell about him, how the queer, soft whistle-whispering would come after me, now here, then there, to confuse me. How he'd creep up on me between the vans or behind the lav tents, how his eyes glistened. How I hated his stumpy dwarf body and old man's head. Rosa had told me once that Little Midge's father had been a true gentleman and that his mother had only one eye – not that the other was blind, there was no other. Just a flat place where an eye should have been. There had been four others in the family like him, cousins and uncles. They had made a fortune at Christmas in panto-mimes.

'Always in demand, rich men.'

'He makes me shudder.'

'The others were clever as paint, but Little Midge was never clever, only cunning.'

It was true he had never touched me, never done anything to me at all but whistle-whisper, and back me up in some corner where I could see his big head and leery old man's face too close and smell his sour breath.

'If I told Da, Da might kill him.'

'It's happened.'

'Da?'

'No. Others. Killings. Scores get settled.'

I knew that was so. There were rows and shouting often enough, women being hit and hitting back. Fights on the open bit away from the vans. People sorted themselves out. But I was Da's future. He had hopes for me. Not that his hopes were my own. They were not. Mine involved quite another sort of life. Rosa knew.

I didn't like the way she was lying, her knees drawn up so tightly. I bent nearer. Without her wig, she looked very old. I had never attached any age to her: age and Rosa had had nothing to do with one another somehow, partly because she lived half of her life in the future, seeing it in the crystal ball and the leaves, and the lines on people's palms, and the other half in the past, listening to the dead, so that there seemed scarcely a time for her to have any existence in the present.

I didn't like her to talk about the dead. It troubled me. I think I even found it embarrassing. I just could never be sure. Rosa respected that, and hardly ever mentioned it.

But now, the future and the past had suddenly changed, telescoped together and shrunk to the now; everything was now, concentrated on a bald old woman curled in a bunk in the oily half-light.

'Do you have a pain in your stomach?'

But she only gave a little groan and pulled herself together more tightly as if she was afraid of coming apart.

Through the slit in the curtain I could see a coloured haze of light from the fairy lamps strung all round the tent. In an hour the crowds would be in for the show. I wondered what Rosa would do, whether she had ever missed an evening before. At the start, and in the interval and again at the end there were always one or two waiting to see her, sometimes a lot more. She had a reputation.

'You read your book,' she said suddenly. 'Yes.'

I didn't need Rosa to tell me that. I read my books in preparation for my own particular future, when I would get away from the racket and the smell and Little Midge's whistle-whisper, and the prospect of marrying one of the Morrises or Alfie the fire-eater.

'Don't you get into trouble . . .'

'Ma knows where I'll be.'

She always did, and complained about it bitterly. I thought she was jealous of the time I spent with Rosa.

'Shouldn't I fetch someone?'

But she rolled her bald head fretfully to and fro on the pillow.

In the end, I got a cup of water and set it by the lamp on the ledge behind her bunk, and made her promise to call if she needed anything.

'I'll hear,' I said, though I never would once the show had begun. I could hear the drum roll practice starting up, and then the sudden blaze of the trumpet. Then the horses began again.

I didn't want to leave her. I hated it. This. It wasn't how things should be in Rosa's van. We hadn't talked, there had been none of her quiet murmuring over the tea leaves. I hadn't sat with my hand, palm up, resting in her dry one, listening. I hadn't told her any stories about the day. We hadn't had a laugh.

She fed off me, I sometimes thought, for a taste of the world outside.

And I didn't want to go out in case Little Midge was here, silkily whistle-whispering. If I waited a bit longer he'd be gone to get ready. I hated him in his spangles and make-up, his old man's face more peculiar than ever, but in the ring he was away from me, under the floodlights, fully visible.

I waited as long as I dared. It was peaceful in Rosa's van, but I didn't feel right, the sense of ease wasn't here. I was jumpy, as if something was about to happen.

Rosa was asleep now. I didn't want to kiss her but I touched her hot forehead. It was dry as a moth.

When I stood up her wig brushed against my face.

The site had that buzz there always is before a show. Van doors opened in your face and people came flying out, in macs and boots over their costumes, trying to dodge the mud and puddles, the horses were all wound up, and Mario's dogs were yapping. The warm-up magic started. This was the time I liked it, the only time, but it churned you up too. It was the danger. There was always that. People could fall. People broke their backs. People had died. I'd heard the stories often enough – ropes giving way, platforms in the roof not secured. The stunt rider who went round and round two feet up, until the day his engine cut out.

Little Midge wasn't there, but I was still jumpy, so that I went up to my calf in muddy water when I heard a whistle behind me, but it was a normal whistle from Johnny Mahoney, carrying his whips under his arm. If there was one person I liked better than any, apart from Rosa, it was Johnny Mahoney. When I was young he used to sit on the top step of his van and tell me Bible stories. He used to say there was always the Boss looking out for me. I had only to give him the nod if I had a problem and he would sort it out. It was something I tried to remember when Little Midge was out there somewhere whistle-whispering.

Johnny Mahoney's wife had died of cancer years before. I hardly remembered her. He kept a shrine to her memory in his van, her photograph among plastic flowers, with a candle in a little ruby-red glass. Her funeral was still talked of as something wonderful to behold – with her name, and a full-size trapeze in white flowers carried on one of the lorries, and every horse and pony wearing black wreaths around their necks, and black ribbons.

'Toodle-oo,' Johnny Mahoney said.

I stopped. I wanted to tell him about Rosa, and for a moment, standing in the rain with my leg soaked in muddy water, I almost did.

But she had said not, and although it troubled me, I had to respect it, so I just said 'Toodle-oo' back, as usual.

Ma was in a pot-banging mood. You could have put a match to the fury in the air. Why it took her was one of the mysteries, and you could never predict when. It was hard to live at close quarters with, so generally I went straight to Rosa's. Now, I just got a glass of water and my book, and went to my bunk, trying to be invisible.

When I lay down, Rosa was in my mind at once. I saw her bald head and her body curled and arched like a caterpillar. The worry of it sat heavy and burning like a coal in the middle of my chest, and I needed to halve the burden of it with someone. But a plate had smashed into the sink and as soon as Da came in the row started, as it was bound to do, she screaming at him, on and on in her own furious unburdening. When I did get to sleep Little Midge's whistle-whisper floated through my dreams.

There are plenty of sentimental stories about people running away to join the circus but I never heard one about the opposite. That night, I came as close as I ever had to going, without warning or preparation, which would have been more than foolish. I knew it had to be planned and done properly. I knew it was not yet.

The other thing that stopped me going was Rosa. I had the responsibility of that.

My neck ached when I woke, I'd been lying so awkwardly, the pillow half over my head. The light was opaque and velvety outside the van windows, which meant a sea mist had rolled up and over the site like a great eiderdown. Da was snoring and the plate was smashed, with the shards all over the sink and the draining board, ready to cut anyone's finger open.

When I stepped outside it was eerie and deathly still. The sea mist touched my face and hair like cobwebs. I picked my way across the mud, feeling my path between the vans. Everybody's curtains were drawn. A dog growled once. Nothing else.

Sometimes here on quiet early mornings you could hear the sea breaking on the rocks far below the cliffs, but not today. It might not have been there.

I almost tripped over the steps of Rosa's van, I could see so little. The mist tasted of rust in my mouth. The steps were sweaty with it, so that I almost slipped.

I knew as soon as I parted the curtains. It was something about the silence. It had a different quality, as though every atom and particle within the van had fallen still and motionless.

I climbed carefully in, not wanting to disturb that stillness. My heart pounded in my ears as fast as castanets.

Only the lamp was still lit on the ledge along the

bunk, and that had burned right down. Rosa was lying on her side almost as I had left her, but her knees were no longer drawn up, and her hand was up close to her face, beneath her cheek.

I knelt down beside her. 'Rosa,' I said.

My voice sounded too loud, breaking open the stillness.

'Rosa.'

I was afraid to touch her at first, but then I did. The moth-wing skin of her forehead was cool. I kissed her, a thing I had never done, never would have thought to do, in her life.

I knew I would have to fetch help, but there was no hurry, and I didn't want people to come crashing into the stillness for good. Once they had, nothing would ever be the same.

It was not the same now.

In the end, I did get up, and felt my way to the door.

'Hoo-ee-ooo. Hoo-ee-oo. Ssssss . . .'

Something rose up inside me then, but it was not fear. It was anger, a fury which I recognised as my mother's. It belonged within us both.

'You stop that and come out here.'

My voice bounced oddly off the billowing sea mist. 'Do you hear me?'

And suddenly, he was there, a yard or two away from me, his flat old man's face opened wide in shock.

'Rosa —' I said, and stopped. I wasn't going to tell him. 'Rosa isn't well. I'm going for someone. You stay here — right here.' I pointed to a position at the bottom of the step. 'You stand guard and don't move — you don't let anyone in there until I come back and you don't go in there yourself. Do you hear?'

He took up the position like a sentry, without speaking.

'Don't you move.'

I plunged into the shroud of mist, in a panic now, to get someone, anyone, to come and take the whole of the burden off me. As I reached the first van, I began to scream.

The sun came out not long after that and the mist rolled back across the flat sea to the horizon. I couldn't escape until late in the afternoon. I had to talk to half the world, but in the end, when it had all stopped, I did go out.

The site had the smell of everybody's tea frying and the kids were sitting in the mud and sun.

The beach was empty, except for some boys a long way off playing cricket, tiny figures on the flat sand. The sea was very quiet, shifting about gently inside itself and creaming at the edge.

I walked and walked and then sat down on some rocks. The seaweed was as green as emeralds, and smelled of fish.

I didn't think about Rosa. I didn't need to. She was there. If I had reached out I could have touched her.

There was one thing I felt bad about. One thing I should have done and that was to have put her wig on for her. People should not have seen her bald like that. I felt I had let her down. Rosa had always had a dignity about her.

I looked along the pale sand. The cricketing boys had gone. This was my place, the only one I had now, and when we moved on, I would not have this calm, secret beach either, until we came back next year.

There was a rock pool behind my foot with a tiny crab sitting in the sand at the bottom. I could see every mark on it through the clear water. I bent down and touched it with my finger and it shrugged itself back at once under the sand and went still.

The sea made its soft sound, turning over and over.

'Hoooo-ee-oo.'

I knew he had stayed guard at the bottom of Rosa's van steps. Johnny Mahoney had told me so. He had done as I had told him, though I could scarcely believe I had ordered him in such a way, but after that I didn't know where he had gone.

'Hoooo-eee-oo.'

The sun had gone off the beach now. I couldn't tell whether he was on the cliff paths above, or behind some of the rocks, he was so clever with his voice.

'Hooo-eee-ooo.'

I began to walk back quickly, though whether I was walking away from Little Midge or towards him I had no way of telling. I thought of what Johnny Mahoney had said. 'Just ask the Boss.'

The cliff path was a long way off. I had walked further than I realised along the beach, further than I had ever gone before.

'Hooo-eee-ooo.'

'Rosa,' I said out loud.

I remembered what they always said in the stories about the old days and the big cats.

'Never turn your back,' was the rule, 'and never run.'

So I didn't run, only walked fast.

'Rosa.'

When I saw the perimeter fence at the edge of the site I started sobbing. My side stabbed where I had pulled a muscle climbing in such a panic up the cliff path. The horses and ponies were whinnying and the dogs were barking. I heard a couple of drum rolls. All the usual racket. I had never been glad of it before.

I didn't want to go past Rosa's van but to avoid it I would have to walk halfway round the site and all the energy and strength had gone out of me like sand out of a timer. Besides, I had to face it so it might as well be now.

And then I saw Little Midge. He was sitting, hunched up on the bottom step of Rosa's van, his big head bent forward into his chest. I stopped dead. He looked as if he had been there for hours. Perhaps all day. Perhaps ever since I had ordered him to stay and not move, in the sea mist of that early morning.

I went nearer, and he heard or sensed me, and looked. I didn't say anything and nor did he, but I saw that he was crying. His old man's face was wet and his eyes were red. He looked like a sad, very old baby. His nose was running and he wiped it on his coat sleeve.

I didn't understand, and then I felt suddenly sick and giddy, so that I would have fainted if I hadn't sat down on the steps of the van next to him. I took some breaths. The world righted itself.

Little Midge smelled of tobacco and musty clothes. I sat there next to him for ages while he went on crying, but I couldn't stand him wiping his nose on his sleeve so in the end I gave him my handkerchief and he used that.

The racket went on all around us. Kids and dogs and drums and horses and van doors opening and shutting. It seemed to have nothing to do with us. We were cut off from it all, sitting on the steps of Rosa's van, having a queer, unspeaking need for one another.

The punishment

The punishment

'Goddit,' Deano said. 'We'll shoot the crucifix.'

They froze as stiff as the plaster saints then and the silence was terrible, as they pictured it in their minds.

'Goddit,' and he banged his fist hard against the breakwater behind them. But he had scared himself as well, they knew that, with the enormity of the idea and that it had come out of him.

The tide was out and there was the usual mean wind.

They looked at the lime-green seaweed smeared over the rocks and the rusty railing sticking out of its sheared-off concrete slab, like a broken bone out of an arm, at the dull sky and the dull sea – anywhere but at each other as what Deano had said sank down into the part of them so deep it might never be reached.

They were already old men, it seemed, by the time Mick bent forward to pick up a pebble and chucked it away from him. The sound when it fell was hardly anything and it made them start as if they were already there and had done the thing, heard the crack of the shot, the church door slam, a sudden voice.

It woke them up though.

'We could,' Deano said, as if they had been shouting him down. 'Simple.'

Mick picked up another pebble. They were only here for him, they were all trying to think of what to do, for him, and because of Charlie, but he was the most fearful of them, that was understood. On the other hand, Charlie had been his brother.

'No,' he said.

'Why not?'

'You know.'

'The worst thing we could think of, you said, except for killing someone, and it's the worst thing.'

'Something might happen.'

'Yea, we'd shoot it and it'd smash to bits.'

It was Sluggy who said the obvious. Sluggy who scarcely spoke, because of the hole in the roof of his mouth that made him sound like an idiot, which he definitely was not.

'No gun.' It came out differently but they never had any trouble understanding him.

'Catapult then.'

'Yea, well.'

But Mick knew when to give in. 'It wouldn't make any noise.' They looked at him. He had given permission. They would do it. He would.

The mean wind blew little pins of rain that stung their faces. Far down the beach, the tide turned.

They got up and went slowly back, not speaking, kicking at the shingle, and the lumps of sand and marran grass beside the path.

'See yer.'

'See yer,' at the usual corner. Only nothing was usual or ever would be again, whether they did it or not. But they would do it. It was as if it had already happened and become a fact, in his life, his past, history, not just a might, and in the future.

'Goddit.'

There was a great hollow, like one of the caves at low tide. It seemed to be just at the back of Mick's mind or behind his head. He dared not look into it. He had to. It had begun to grow from the bubble that had formed there the moment Deano had said it. 'We'll shoot the crucifix.' And Mick had known at once that they would.

Everything filled it as it grew, it became crowded with thickening, shifting shapes. Hellfire, though, strangely, there were no flames. A stench, of sulphur and incense. Mary and the saints. The plaster statues weeping paint blood and the red holes on the plaster feet, the open, wounded heart. His own white shirt and black bow tie on elastic and the mesh of marks on his knees from pressing into the altar carpet at his First Communion. His mother's face behind the short black veil. Father O'Connell's mumbling voice on the other side of the confessional box. Angels. Words.

'Who made you?'

'God made me.'

'Why did God make you?'

'God made me to know him, love him and serve him in this world and to be happy with him for ever in the next.'

He was walking faster and faster, banging his feet hard onto the pavement as he went up the steep hill towards the Bracken, working himself up into a boiling of fear. But more than the fear ever could be was the anger that filled up the black cave, blotting out everything else there and growing until he thought his head would burst.

The punishment

The way it happened might have been expected. Charlie's mouth had always got the better of him; none of them could have counted the number of times one of the fathers had said, 'Your tongue will be the death of you, Charlie Coghlan,' though never thinking it could actually come true. There were just the kept-behinds, the raw knuckles from the ruler and burning red legs from the strap, and he never learned, never thought before he came out with something, nor ever seemed to put the cause and the punishment together to make two. Mick had given up on him long before.

It had been quick.

'Twenty-seven point four multiplied by nine.' The yellow-stained forefinger had stabbed at Charlie, who was silent, slumped down in his seat. The priest had come round. Mick, in the desk behind, caught the swish of the black habit.

'Twenty-seven point four by nine.' He had taken hold of Charlie's ear hard between the yellowed fingers. He had long fingernails, which Mick thought a man should not have.

'Geddoff, bugger you.' Charlie had wrenched his

head away and Mick's heart had stopped like a lift with the ropes severed. Then the classroom exploded.

After the beating, the punishment had gone on for the rest of the week. Every night, he was kept in and on the Friday longer than ever. Mick waited more than an hour before going to find him.

The school joined up to the presbytery, with gardens in between crossed by paths where the priests walked, holding the black book up to their faces saying the office. At the back was the kitchen garden, the sheds, the sagging wire netting around the chicken house.

'Uh.'

'I'm looking for my brother.'

'Uh.'

The fat bald brother who kept the bees and potatoes and hens was toothless and deaf, more difficult to understand even than Sluggy. He knew what Mick wanted though, always knew.

Mick followed him. Once he turned and his white moon face held a terrible sadness. He knew why in the shed. The brother had piled up crates to sit Charlie down on, and another for him to rest his foot. The foot was red, the whole of it, and on the floor

were a wet scarlet sock and plimsoll. Charlie had his
arms tight round his chest, as if to hold himself
together, and he was rocking to and fro and making
an odd little mewling noise.

'Uh.'

The fork had gone right through his foot. The
brother had pulled it out and brought him in from
where Charlie had been digging, put him here and
fetched a bucket of water.

'I didn't know,' Mick said. 'How could I?'

Charlie went on holding himself together, rocking
to and fro, to and fro, inside the sour-smelling
chicken shed, with the slats of dusty light falling onto
his hands and the egg crates and the scarlet sock and
plimsoll.

It had taken Mick more than an hour to get him
home somehow, and Charlie another four days to die,
in terror and maddening fever from the poison that
blackened his foot, blowing it up to three times its
size, then racing up through him like the tide,
drowning him.

Mick had gone in to see him and his face had been
odd, twisted out of shape and bloated, like the corpses

of the fish left rotting at low tide. It wasn't Charlie's face.

Their mother sat sponging him, dipping her left hand into the enamel bowl of Holy Water and letting it trickle over his forehead and cheeks and run down into his neck.

Mick had stood twisting the loose door handle about. Neither of them had looked at him.

Later that day, a Sister of Mercy had come, a crow flapping slowly up the stairs, and Mick had sat with his back against the banister hearing the soft murmur of the prayers, the voices going up and down in rhythm and the click of the rosary.

He had closed his eyes then, dropped his head and prayed with a raging passion he had never even known the shadow of before. 'Make him not die. Make him not die. Make him not die.'

He knew it was not a proper prayer, like the prayers being recited by his mother and the Sister of Mercy, it was more, far more.

'*Make him not die.*'

But Charlie had. The hatred and rage in Mick's heart were terrifying and which was the strongest, towards God, or himself, or the priest with the yellow forefinger, he could not have said.

The others had caught the rage from him. They were like brothers anyway, and now even more so — but impotent, somehow, until Deano had said that.

'Goddit. We'll shoot the crucifix.'

Two days later he went to Deano's house, at the other end of the Bracken, which was just a block of five dirty white houses joined together and set down as if they had been dropped out of the sky from nowhere, and around them was only scrub and an old square of hardcore where there had once been Nissen huts.

The back door of Deano's was open and the smell met you with the flies. He was used to it, though it still always choked him. They left raw meat in slabs on the floor for the dogs and open tins of sardines with forks stuck in.

'Hiya.'

No one turned round. The little dark room was full of them, and all the same, with skinny dirty necks and skinny long arms.

On the plastic tablecloth they'd rigged up a cross of broken sticks punched into a lump of putty. The real

crucifix was on the mantelpiece between two candle-
sticks and a bunch of plastic flowers.

Mick watched. Norrie held the catapult up quite
high, squinting down his nose. He had a cigarette
stuck to his lower lip.

'Pow.'

But the stone skidded onto the floor.

'Give it here.'

At the end of an hour they were good, but Mick
was best and couldn't miss. They drifted out of the
house and sat on the back step, except Norrie, who
posed by the fence, eyes half-closed against his
cigarette smoke. 'Can't miss.'

They looked at Mick.

'No,' he said.

'You got to.'

'It was Deano's idea.'

They didn't bother to answer. The words about
Charlie being his brother just hung like Norrie's
smoke on the air. The vengeance was his, by rights.

Norrie flicked his stub into the pile of broken
bicycles. 'Right.'

Mick was almost out of the gate before Deano said,
'Saturday night. Eleven o'clock.' He hardly raised his

voice but Mick was so strung up he'd have heard a whisper half a mile away.

The bad thing was he couldn't say any prayers about it, so there was no help from anywhere. After Charlie, he knew that prayers might not work, but they'd still seemed possible and now they were not.

He avoided the others and didn't go near the breakwater, or to the other end of the Bracken.

Once his mother said, 'Haven't you got more to do than hang about here?' in the old way, and the next second he saw the flicker over her face, the wish that she could bite back what she'd said. After Charlie she had sworn never again to say it, never to push him out of the house, never give him another tongue-lashing.

After Charlie, like everything. But it couldn't have lasted and he was relieved because it felt normal again.

She had opened her purse. 'Take it. Buy some chips. Go to the Amusements. Why not?' She held out the guilt offering. He hated to look into her face, still shocked that eyes could change so completely, still appalled by the sadness.

He took the coin. He should have kissed her and could not.

They were allowed anywhere except for Fun Land, which was not in the open, but down steep steps underground, a place like a cave, smelling of damp. You didn't know who might be hanging about down there and the air was bad, she said, and neither he nor Charlie had ever minded being forbidden to go, afraid of the look of it, opening at their feet like the mouth of hell, with orange and green sulphur lights and awful, echoing, shrieking voices.

But now he went straight there without hesitating or letting himself think or imagine, ran down the steps and paid to go through the turnstile.

And it was hell, as he had known it would be, and beckoning and exciting and terrifying as hell must be. The noise of the dodgem cars bounced off the walls and the electricity at the tips of their trailing poles fizzed and sparked.

He could hear the shots and went straight for them. No one else was at the stand. The line of ducks bobbed along past him and round the back and came bobbing round again, and each time he took aim he had only to think of Charlie and his swollen bruise-coloured face, or the scarlet sock and plimsoll shining wet on the shed floor.

The ghost train screamed and howled behind its shocking hoardings and the laugh of the maniac policeman rang in his head, and he was in hell and triumphant, he could not miss. Crack. Could not. Crack. Crack. Crack.

The electric-blue nylon rabbit was huge and burned his fingers, he could scarcely hold it to run up the steps and across the Bay Road, and throw it over the railing into the sea. The tide was high, and turning.

'Can't miss.'

All he had to do was think of Charlie.

'Can't miss.'

Which was the worst of it now, that he could not, and was damned because of it.

He ran home to exhaust himself and not be able to think, but it was all there waiting for him at the bottom of the steps into the darkness of sleep, the open mouth of hell and the spit and hiss and the screaming. There was a grinning clown's head on a turntable, with wide-parted scarlet lips between which you threw plastic balls.

'Can't miss.'

He threw and threw and could not; even when he threw them up into the air, or away behind him, somehow the mouth caught and swallowed them each time.

Waking, he lay quite calmly, with one question in his mind. What would happen? After he had not missed. *What would happen?*

Slipping out was easy. The doctor had given his mother tablets after Charlie, and she still took them. He just stayed in his clothes, sitting on his bed and hardly breathing, until half-past ten, and then went, leaving the lights off and the back door on the latch.

There was enough of a moon, lumpy and pumpkin-coloured, to see by. Mick slid close to the hedges, fences, walls.

There was no getting out of it. It was the right time, long after confessions were over and the priests had finished preparing the altar for early Mass. No one would be there.

Charlie, he thought, and said his name out,

'Charlie, Charlie, Charlie'. His foot had gone black where the poison had filled and swollen the flesh. He had not recognised anyone.

But now, for the first time, Mick could not picture Charlie. He saw everything else – the chicken run, the deaf and dumb brother's soft open mouth and anxious eyes, the electric-blue nylon rabbit, even a mushroom night-light he had had by his bed until he was three.

Not Charlie. He tried to force the pictures of him to switch on in his head but they would not come. He thought he might have lost them for ever then.

Two shadows, merging with the gateposts.

'Mick.'

They just touched each other. Sluggy's face looked dark and flat in the peculiar moonlight.

'I didn't tell Norrie.'

No. This was nothing to do with Norrie, rat's-tail thin, worldly.

They had not needed to plan how to get into the church, they knew well enough, and went in file round the side to the door no one used. The priests went in at the other side, at the end of the path leading from the presbytery.

Sluggy was the smallest and lightest and went in easily, up onto Deano's shoulder and, after a second or two of fiddling at the inside catch, snaking through, while Mick held his legs and feet until the exact last moment before letting him drop. It wasn't far. The bolts made too much noise and the key was stiff, the waiting there in the darkness made them old men; Mick could smell Deano's dirty smell, the smell of his home.

Then time reeled them in again, as Sluggy opened the door.

It was another smell. He had never understood how they mattered. All the stale incense and snuffed candle smoke of his life came into his nostrils, making his head spin, whispering to him each word he had ever learned by heart. The Catechism. The Mass. The Sacred Heart. The Holy Trinity. 'Forgive me, Father, for I have sinned', 'Hail Mary, full of grace . . .', 'Glory be to the Father . . .'

'Jesus.'

They clutched at each other, standing in the great black hollow ribcage of the empty church. Above the altar, the red glow of the Reserved Sacrament.

'The body and blood of our Lord Jesus Christ preserve your body and soul into everlasting life.'

'No way.'

The whisper hissed out like a snake's tongue into the incensed darkness.

But then, when he had given up all hope of ever seeing him again, he saw Charlie, and not Charlie blackened and swollen with his eyes rolling in his head, but Charlie standing up straight and laughing into his face, Charlie waving both arms above his head, blazing, triumphant.

Mick let go of Deano's arm and walked forward down the side aisle, between the pews, and up again until he was at the foot of the altar steps.

It was not black dark, only dim. He focused on the flickering ruby light. The others were behind him, close to his shoulder.

He waited a long time, until his heart had slowed down, wiping his palm several times on his shirt. Then he reached behind him and Deano put the catapult and the stone into his hand.

'Mick —' but he didn't bother finishing it. He knew it was all right.

With Charlie just ahead of him, still laughing, Mick

went up the three shallow concreted steps, and stood in front of the altar a few feet from the crucifix. At his shoulder, Deano switched on the torch and focused the beam.

Charlie was still laughing.

What would happen?

But now something changed, though only for a fragment of a second. Now, instead of rage, he felt an extraordinary and overwhelming sadness; it raced up through him like the tide, filled him, drowned him in itself, and then ran back until he was left empty and stranded, trembling. He waited. Charlie laughed again.

The sound of the stone as it hit the brass crucifix, and then of the crucifix as it hit the stone floor behind the altar, cracked out like cymbals and went on cracking round and round inside the hollow darkness, wave after wave. It was the end of the world and the veil of the temple was rent in two, everything came down on them. The crash of brass grew fainter and fainter. Stopped. They waited for the row from the street outside and the breaking down of the door. The marching men and the torches.

There was only silence, and after a second the

squeak of a plimsoll as Sluggy moved his foot suddenly.

Charlie was fading now, he could hardly make him out.

From habit he genuflected, crossed himself and turned away from the altar. Deano clicked the torch off so that the darkness blinded him.

They parted from Sluggy at the corner, and he and Deano walked all the way to the Bracken without speaking. Deano evaporated into the darkness there, and even then neither of them spoke a word.

The back door was just as he had left it. The house still. The latch jumped down too loudly into its socket, but no one woke.

He had thought that he would never sleep again, but he slept at once and dreamed nothing. He had thought Mass would be late and the crucifix missing, with a different one put in its place, but Father O'Connell came out onto the altar as the bell stopped on the minute of eight and the great brass cross was upright and shining as it caught the sun, the splayed figure unharmed.

He had thought there would be mention made, an

inquest, an appeal for those responsible. But the sermon was about spreading the gospel through the missions to Communist China and nothing was said.

He had thought his legs might not bear him up in the line for Holy Communion and the host burst into flames as it touched his tongue, but he moved up behind his mother as usual and the host tasted of wallpaper and was cool in his mouth.

He did not look for the others. Anyway, Deano often missed. He had a different sort of mother.

Father O'Connell put out his hand, greeting them at the porch, and Mick had to take the yellow fingers but the look on his face was no different and nothing happened, nothing was said.

Which, in the end, was the worst of it. Nothing happened. Nothing ever happened and for the rest of his life he was waiting and the fear was always there, a cold, hard, bitter pebble lodged in his chest, cold but at the same time blazing red and burning into him.

He and Deano and Sluggy hung about by the breakwater and at the corner of the Bracken and occasionally at Deano's house, where the smell was still terrible. Norrie turned holy for a while and even thought of going for a priest, but ended up staying at home, forever half-closing his eyes against his cigarette smoke, his teeth rotten and always giving him grief and a foul temper.

Sluggy moved away after the operation on the hole in his mouth and they never knew whether it had made him talk better.

Mick took to carpentry and liked it, then threw it up, went south, married, left her, traipsed about, never settled. Never could. Because of the waiting and the fear and the dreams of the hollow, incensed darkness and the feel of the stone in the palm of his hand and the sound of the brass crashing down, crashing on and on and on. He took up smoking but it didn't help, because nothing could. All that would help would be when something happened to punish him and put an end to it.

'Goddit. We'll shoot the crucifix.'

He often heard Deano saying it, and the thump of his fist against the wet wood of the breakwater, and waited, for the consequence of it all.

He thought that almost certainly the waiting would kill him by itself, but it didn't, and after a time he simply accepted that it never would but that he would die of something very ordinary, like old age.

Until then, he just had to wait, and go on waiting while nothing happened. Nothing at all.

Moving messages

Moving messages

Some people make tunes, but it is lines that run like moving messages through my head. Whatever else I am saying and doing often has no bearing on this inner, verbal life.

'Thou hast made me, and shall thy work decay?'

It rode with me up the escalator and my footsteps tapped it out in a rhythm along the street. My mother had a similar problem with hymns.

'I am a little world made cunningly.'

I wondered if Velma had ever suffered from poetic tinnitus. It might provide an opening.

The restaurant was chrome and black and angular and a shock to the system. The table was square, the plates were square and the water came in a square glass, but the bread rolls were round and soft, like my life now, lived among hills like breasts and tender bales of fabric.

They had tortured flowers with wire stays, and

straitjacketed them in thin metal tubes. The table napkins were origami.

'Didi!'

Her kiss scratched my cheek, dry as a quill.

'Goodness,' I said. I have not been Didi for thirty-four years.

I had painted Velma in my mind and the picture had been a good likeness. She was blade-thin, wore cream, smoked.

'You look so wholesome,' she said. 'London is foul.'

The menus were startling, scarlet boards lettered in spikes of black.

'Shall I order for us both?'

They say we do not see ourselves as others see us, but I saw perfectly how Velma saw me and I was not having it.

'Crab,' I said, speaking directly to the waiter. 'Turbot with buttered spinach. Pommes dauphinoise.'

'Six gulls' eggs, and a tiny salad.'

Velma lit a cigarette.

'You used to smoke Black Russian,' I said. It had been a matter for wonder among the rest of us.

'I'd have known you,' I said.

I meant, you look your age and more, look harder, smarter, slicker, dryer; look like this restaurant. Yet, oddly, still the same. They can do this sort of thing with computers now. Digital ageing.

The hills like breasts and the soft folds of fabric and pillows of fabric have had an effect on me, too.

'*Thou hast made me, and shall thy work decay?*'

'Known you anywhere,' I said.

The crab tasted of seaside holidays and flaked sweetly between my teeth.

'Extraordinary.'

I wondered what, but she said it while looking round at two men who were walking into the restaurant. In fact I was not sure she had meant to speak to me at all, and buttered a soft, plump roll to fill in time. It is not every day I eat in a cutting-edge London restaurant with square plates.

'*I am a little world made cunningly,*' the moving message read, neon-green on black. 'I need intellectual discipline,' I said, though how could she have understood? 'Fierce words. Analysis.'

That was probably the reason for the tinnitus.

In a train, when you are facing the moving message about not leaving personal belongings behind you it is possible to raise a newspaper to shut it out, but I have found no similar way of dealing with the lines inside my head. I should have asked my mother what she did about the hymns, whether she simply let Wesley flow reassuringly, upliftingly on.

'Aren't gull's eggs very dry?' I said.

I caught Velma's expression as I lifted a forkful of steaming, buttery spinach and potato to my mouth.

I was everything she could patronise. I laid the forkful of food down uneaten on the square plate. At home I eat square boxes of soup and too much butter and live among full-breasted hills, and bales of soft fabric.

The turbot was glutinous and very white on the black plate.

Velma patted cigarette ash into the broken shells of her gulls' eggs.

'I daresay you've made a lot of money, too,' I said.

We ought to begin the conversation about the past now, the one we had almost begun on the telephone.

'No, don't tell me, let's meet . . .'

She had rung up the magazine that featured my quilts among the soft-breasted hills, and briskly obtained my number.

'Do you remember Douglas Merton? He became a bishop. Do you remember Georgina Lee? She's a prison governor. And a dame,' I said. 'Imagine. Imagine.'

A smaller scarlet card was flourished, the spiked lettering in silver this time, making the puddings quite hard to decipher.

When I looked up squinting from the parfaits and coulis and tartes, I saw that Velma was crying. They were discreet tears, and quite silent, caught trembling in the spider legs of mascara.

'Oh God. What can I do? I must be able to do something. What can I order? Shall I order you brandy?' I said.

'Dear Didi.' Cream, thin, hard, dry, smart, weeping Velma. 'Practical Didi.'

So then I did order brandy, which came with my softly mounded, smooth, shining, rose-red mousse, stuck with horizontal chocolate quills, like a chic hat on a plate.

'I've no idea, really,' I said, 'what you *do*.'

'Recruitment.' Velma finished her brandy in one impressive swallow. 'Until I sold the company.'

To one side of the rose-red hat was a small sphere of glistening rose-pink ice.

'But mainly, I'm a mistress.'

Do you remember Velma Prescott? She's a mistress now. Imagine.

But the spider-legs of mascara had released the tears, which slid down her porcelain cheekbones, until I wanted to cry with her.

'Brandy makes it worse,' I said.

My ice tasted intensely of lavender.

'*I am a little world made cunningly*.'

'Has he left you, or something?'

Almost an hour later, nervy with three tiny pewter-coloured cups of bitter coffee, I had learned that he had not. I had learned almost everything.

After the restaurant, we had walked a long way and then sat down on a backless bench in a churchyard, though if I had worn such a suit as Velma's I would never have done that. But Velma was immersed in trying to stop herself crying, rather as one is in trying to stop a nosebleed. I had no helpful suggestions, so I looked at the tombstones.

('At the round earths imagin'd corners, blow Your trumpets, Angells.')

I welcomed the moving messages now, feeling a desperate need for the bracing sustenance of words.

'It was seeing you,' Velma said. 'In that magazine.'

The tears seemed to have dried.

'There you sat. That view, all that wonderful coloured stuff tumbling off your lap. I haven't slept properly since.'

'Winter in the country can be quite testing,' I said.

Two buses roared past the churchyard, rows of faces peering down at us, round, white Os, such as children draw.

'We got buses a lot, in those days,' I said.

'I still do.'

I stared.

'The underground is filthy.'

I stared.

'What did you think, then – the Bentley and the chauffeur?'

Like sudden sunlight, the old Velma shone out. Looking at her next to me on the green, backless bench, I decided she had not, after all, had a facelift.

We were fifty-four. Flesh and skin and hair betray us.

(*'Thou hast made me, and shall thy work decay?'* I made a vow then, to embrace the old disciplines. The words.)

We had been incongruous, unexpected friends from our first day, without anything but English Literature and twenty-three other students in common.

'I don't think I could accommodate my life to someone else,' I said, 'on their terms. Not even for all the accounts at Knightsbridge shops.'

She had told me everything about it, before my edible millinery had arrived. She had a taxi account, a dress account, a hair account, even a flower account.

'Wives can wear slippers and tracksuits,' she had said. 'Mistresses can't. Their hair must always be immaculate, make-up applied and the flowers must never have dead petals. And of course although I suppose an unavoidable major illness might be forgiven, colds are out.'

'Wherever,' I said, 'is the benefit?'

We both looked at the word money as it ran past us, a silent, moving message.

A thin little wind had got up and scattered bits of paper about the churchyard.

'I can't tackle London often,' I said; 'you need your wits about you.'

Still, I was sharpening up now. I did not want to leave. I was not missing the soft-breasted hills and the fabrics in any way.

'It is just – uncreative,' Velma said. 'There is nothing to show for it.'

'I am a little world made cunningly.'

'As a matter of fact,' I said to Velma, 'I have been thinking about a higher degree. There is nothing furthering to the cause of human endeavour in quilts.'

A plastic cup had fetched up against my ankle.

Perhaps I meant it. The texts were there, I knew most of the words, I'd been saving them up on the moving messages.

'But you looked so right,' Velma said. 'Dear Didi.'

She wanted me in my place. I saw that.

She was older again and there were no marks at all on her cream suit from the green backless bench.

'Dear Didi.'

I felt confused emotions. Angry. Patronised. Dissatisfied.

131

I kicked the plastic cup hard across the path.

The green country that led towards the soft-breasted hills looked queer and different from the windows of the train. Strange, unfamiliar and unnerving. I did not know if I liked it any more. But when I thought of the angular restaurant and the dark churchyard I did not like those either.

'*I am a little world made cunningly.*'

It was raining when I got back, and the cloud was low and draped in scarves about the soft-breasted hills.

'*At the round earths imagin'd corners.*'

Velma would be dressed in taupe and pearls, made up, among the immaculate flowers.

'*Thou hast made me, and shall thy work decay?*'

'There is nothing to show for it,' Velma had said. 'It is just − uncreative.'

I let myself into the house and stood, among the bales of fabric in the last grey light. '*Blow Your trumpets, Angells.*'

I watched the moving messages for some time. I was grateful for them. They might mean nothing and

lead nowhere. But Velma did not have them. I was
sure of that.

So I supposed I was to be envied.

Sand

Sand

Their mother's father had been a saint. He had died before he was forty of an illness he had accepted without complaint, which made him a martyr too. Lizzie and Clara had only one picture of him in their minds, from a story their mother told and re-told, of him sitting beside the stove in the evenings with the two dogs asleep at his feet. At nine he would take out his pocket watch to wind, yet twenty seconds before he made the slightest movement, without fail the dogs got up and ran to the door.

They went to their own beds at night with the picture of the uncomplaining invalid and the telepathic dogs in their minds as they lay down.

But their mother's mother was never spoken about, though they had known that she still existed, 'with Aunt Kath'.

They were afraid of their mother, even years after they had homes of their own. There were subjects they had never raised, questions they had never asked and now never could.

After the funeral they had looked, horrified at their own daring, in the green leather hat box in case they might find a will, and had not, though they found their own birth certificates and some school reports, but nothing that went back into her past, or was connected only with her rather than with all of them. The hat box had been mysterious, anything might have been inside, they had believed in it as they might have believed in a fabled casket or a piece of the True Cross, and now it had been exposed and it was nothing, after all, a hollow drum.

Clara put the lid back and for a moment, kneeling on the floor in the fading January light, either of them might have begun a conversation that could have continued for the rest of their lives. The house was very still and filled with their mother as well as with her coats and shoes and the silk kimono Lizzie had so unsuitably brought her back from a single visit abroad. Seeing it hanging, never worn, scarcely even so much as touched, behind the bedroom door, had brought the flush of shame to her face all over again.

'We ought to put the light on,' Lizzie said.

But they did not move, and now the others seemed to press in upon them with the gathering dark, the grandmother they had never been allowed to see or so much as mention, the Aunt Kath who sent them their joint birthday card, without any word of greeting written, just that name 'Aunt Kath', the grandfather, saint and martyr, and the telepathic dogs.

Listening now in the cold front room, they might have heard the winding of the pocket watch.

They could barely see one another's faces.

'Do you remember the handkerchief?' Clara said and her voice in the silent room among the ghosts, made them start and glance around. They did not put the light on, but, lent courage by the darkness, by each other's presence and the growing acceptance that she was dead, they allowed themselves then to be drawn on a few steps into the tunnel mouth of memory.

'The boy,' Clara said.

They would not go to the beach. Then, after all, they might. They would. Might not. Perhaps. And so it had gone on, their hopes swung violently about, and though they were quite used to it, still they had never built up any defences against such disappointments. The truth, which they had never understood, was that their mother was unwilling to make herself uncomfortable for them, resenting as she did what they had already and inevitably cost her.

She did not like the beach, which they were not allowed to call 'the sands'. It would be too hot there, or too cold or too windy, or else a mist would roll in off the sea, or it was the weekend and too crowded, or a weekday and too bleak. But they did not learn because they could not, only continued to hope and have their hopes extinguished, only went on and on in spite of it, clamoured to go.

But then, quite suddenly, though it was a Saturday and would be crowded and August and quite hot, the moment after they had given up hope and spilled a dull game with counters onto this same carpet in this same front room, she had got up and said they would go, now, they were to hurry up, hurry up, if they wanted to come at all, and they had hurried, never daring to catch one another's eye, for fear it might not be true and they would wake and find themselves still here with the game of counters after all.

Of course it had been hopeless. The only deckchair left had been at the wrong end of the beach, too near the shellfish stalls, and a wind had got up, a hot wind, which was the most unhealthy and there had been a plague of flies. They had rushed through the creaming browny-coloured foam at the water's edge and on into the sea, and then, on some unspoken signal, like the signal obeyed by the grandfather's telepathic dogs, they had turned their backs on her, though they could not quite forget, not immediately, or ever properly turn their backs on, her discontent. They were already old enough now to feel guilty, as if what made her discontented were their fault; and at the same time to be resentful, knowing they were not, could not possibly be guilty, though that was never to leave them for the rest of their lives and did not end with her death – nor had they expected that it would.

They were forbidden to talk to other children, 'people we don't know', but there were some girls and one small boy and they began to jump through the waves and shriek with them and after a while they all splashed one another, though not a word was spoken by Lizzie or Clara, so that they were able to believe that none of it counted.

And then, racing along the water's edge, away and away, with their backs to the fish stalls and the deckchair, suddenly they forgot her, and a great and wonderful brightness entered them and lifted them up and the brilliance of the day and the expanse of silver sea dazzled them and the whole feeling somehow entered deep into them, it went into their eyes and was absorbed by their skin, it became part of them and their memories and even, somehow, of their souls, so that now, kneeling across the open leather hat box in the darkness, the feeling washed up over them and through them, transfiguring them again.

As soon as they had turned to go back of course they had seen her, standing up and waving and waving them to come in. She was too hot or blown about, there would be too many flies or the wrong sort of people, she was restless or bored or all those things, but they did not care which, it did not matter to them. It was over, that was all, and long, long before they were ready, though not before they expected.

They had trailed as slowly as they dared back up the beach, to the misery of having damp feet, grainy with sand, pushed into their shoes. Perhaps it was sand she hated most, sand other people had walked over and delved into and dug about and buried things in. Sand was not only ground-up rocks and the pounded bones of thousand-year-old fish; sand might be anything. She rubbed them with the hard little sandy towel and sand scraped their skin – 'Like sandpaper,' Clara said, with a flash of understanding.

It was because of sand that they had met the boy, as they walked slowly back, up the narrow slope from the foreshore. Old dry sand always collected along the gutters and even they could see that this sand was not clean and would never in a thousand years have touched it. It was mixed with black grit and people trod in it with their shoes on, dogs peed and did their dirt into it. It was this sand now that came swirling down the slope, wrapped around chip paper and cigarette butts on a funnel of hot wind, and in the middle of trying to dodge it and not drop their buckets and spades and cardigans, they saw the boy.

The sand had been blown into his eyes, he was howling, his nose was running, and they had made to do what they always must and hurry past, heads bent and looking the other way, whatever they felt about his crying and pain and misery from the blown sand, however they might think about it later, in bed after their light had been switched out, and be ashamed. But their mother had hesitated and then, striking them to stone, gone over to the boy, who wore plimsolls without laces.

'It hurts . . . me eyes hurt.'

They had watched as she had behaved towards him in a way so entirely new to them they could not meet one another's glances for the strangeness of it. She had got him to stop rubbing the sand deeper into his eyes before tipping his head back with her hand beneath his chin.

'Mam, Mam.'

'Where is your mother?'

'At the bus. I has to go there.'

He had roared again, dragging his arm across his nose.

'Where is your handkerchief?'

She spoke to him like a teacher, they thought, raising her voice as if he were very stupid.

'Ain't got handkerchief.'

Nothing more astonishing could happen, but then it did. She had opened her bag and from the special compartment at the back where it was always kept, she had taken the sacred relic. Clara had reached for Lizzie's hand in a sort of terror.

The handkerchief had belonged to the saint and martyr, it was sacred, never used, never so much as touched, though sometimes spoken of. 'It is all I have of my father.'

It was white with a monogram and a blue border, folded and pressed into a perfect square.

Now, their mother took one corner of the sacred relic, screwed it round into a twist and then began to probe at the blown sand and grit in the corners of the boy's eyes, and when she had finished, they saw that he was staring at the white cloth, no longer blinded, as if the handkerchief had worked a miracle. They had already felt peculiar, almost as if they might faint, but after that, nothing could ever surprise them again, so that it seemed quite unremarkable that she should be giving him the handkerchief.

'Tell your mother to send it back laundered.'

He was holding the cool, healing piece of linen not just to his smarting eyes now but spread out over his whole face.

'Do you hear me?'

He nodded.

'What is your name?'

'Lenny.'

'What are you to do, Lenny?'

'Mam's to send it back.'

'Mrs Murgatroyd. 35 Victoria Avenue. Say it.'

He said it. They heard their own address spoken aloud but it did not seem to have any meaning for them, the words made sounds that were not language at all.

And then he had gone, racing away down the steep path, the handkerchief still held close to his filthy face, and they went on clutching one another's hands for fear everything else would change entirely and that they might find themselves transformed or even dead.

'Well? Hurry up.' She was ahead of them, almost at the top of the slope, before their own legs would unlock and move as they told them.

No word was spoken until they were in their beds.

'What else might happen?' Clara said.

There was silence again, in which each tried to imagine some unimaginable change in their mother, brought about by the boy.

'I touched it once,' Lizzie said. And straight away they could feel the relic between their fingertips in the darkness, the softness and smoothness of the sacred cotton.

They tried to picture it, wherever it was with the boy, but the place was dark and quite undeterminable, they failed entirely and so almost at once they slept, exhausted by the strain of imagining, like mediums drained by the demands of the other world.

None of it had been referred to again. Things were just as they had been, there were no more surprises and by this they were quite unsurprised. After a month the incident came to seem quite unreal to them and more unlikely than a dream.

The room was not dark because the orange street-light had come on and showed them one another's faces, but it was very quiet and in a different way now, as if the ghosts had retreated. The space between them was quite empty.

'I found the handkerchief,' Clara said at last. 'After they took her away. I went to put her clean bed jacket in the drawer.'

Neither could sense the other breathing.

'It was at the back. I left it there.'

And at once their minds leapt to the sacred relic again and found it, at once their hands went out to touch it.

Months had gone by, it had been after Christmas, they had quite forgotten the summer or that it had ever been possible to run in sunshine on the beach. Then it had come, a smeared brown envelope dropped through the letterbox onto the mat. Their mother had bent over it, staring down, before lifting it carefully by one corner.

It was the same envelope in the drawer now. They pictured the thick, unformed lettering: 'Mrs. 35 Victoria Ave' and the town. No surname. He must not have remembered.

There was nothing else, no note. Nothing except the handkerchief, laundered and folded.

She had turned her head. 'What are you doing there?'

They had fled.

When they got back from school it had gone and was never referred to, might never have been at all, and afterwards they almost came to believe that that was so, that the handkerchief did not exist any more than the boy had existed, any more than their mother had, for a few minutes, been utterly transformed.

Elizabeth

Elizabeth

Every day, as soon as they got in, they had to put their wet things on the rack above the stove, and their boots upside down on newspaper, to drain. But this summer was dry, and so already marked out to them as different.

'The sun has shone for nine days,' Milo said, and there was suspicion, as well as wonder, in his voice.

He scuffed at the dust that lay along the gutter.

Minchy Fagin was standing at the corner of the green, by the petrol pump; the canvas bag over his shoulder heaved slightly.

'Don't you get near,' Elizabeth said, and pulled at her brother's arm. She could sense his passionate interest, concealed, but to her keen and clear as a whistle, directed towards Minchy Fagin. (Though it was she who had the ferrety dreams, of chiselled yellow teeth and red eyes.)

'Your Da and Ma came by,' Minchy Fagin said.

Elizabeth pulled again at Milo's arm.

'You're hurting me, Elizabeth.'

'You keep walking on.'

'Your Da and Ma in the truck. On their way to town, weren't they?'

Fatally then, she hesitated. 'On their way to see the doctor. Mary Hennessy said. She was there, in the waiting room.'

She had heard it now.

'Elizabeth . . .'

She began to walk away very quickly, head up, staring straight ahead, and he was stumbling to keep up, and hold his school bag, and rub his arm where she had gripped him like pincers. He knew his sister's strength and authority, could see them now in the set of her shoulders.

It was almost a mile home, from where the bus dropped them. The village straggled out along the road.

'Elizabeth!'

She did pause then, hearing the fear in his voice.

'Will everything be all right at home?'

'Oh yes.'

'How do you know? It might not be. How do you know?'

The sweet had paper and fluff matted to it. It had been for weeks in her pocket.

'Yes!'

His face went bland and soft with pleasure, as his tongue folded round the sweet. She had not been ready for his questioning. Her own anxiety was too much upon her, like a shadow fallen. No one in their family went sixteen miles to see Doctor Hennessy, for just nothing. The last time she had been taken, it was to have him lance a boil between her shoulderblades, that would not be drawn even with the hottest poultice, and had kept her sitting up, and crying with pain, for three nights. Even then, they had gone there on the bus, with every jolt and jar an agony. Da would not take time off to drive them in the truck.

The sun shone hard in their faces, and the sky was muzzed with the heat. Even days like this were long remembered and talked about, but to have weeks of sun, without the familiar, soft grey veils of rain, drifting over them from the hills, gave her a feeling of strangeness in itself.

After Christmas, she would be twelve. Thinking of that troubled her, she wanted to clutch at everything familiar and hold it to her. But the heat and dryness were not familiar, and now, there was this new anxiety.

Yet the house, when they went in through the back door, seemed the same, and its smell was a comfort. There was the jug of cold tea on the table beside the loaf, and a ticking silence about the place.

'Elizabeth? You come and help me now, would you be good?'

She was picking the beans that hung down, heavy, from the row of canes. Elizabeth pushed her way through the ropy tangle of stems to the inside of them, where the light was undersea green. She dropped the picked beans into her lifted skirt. The leaves smelled bitter. She felt Ma's presence on the other side of the green curtain, saw the faded patch of her skirt; she could have reached out and touched her. She crouched down, and this, too, was childhood – being small among the beans. This smell.

'They say it's not been so hot for a hundred years.'

'They do.'

'We saw Minchy Fagin, by the pumps.'

Silence. But there had been a fraction's pause in the picking.

Elizabeth crawled out from under the canes,

holding up her laden skirt. Ma stood lower down the row. Her hands were still on the beans, her eyes far away. It seemed important not to interrupt. But in the moment of looking, Elizabeth had a flash of insight, like a vision, and in it, she understood what it was to be poor, and hard-worked, with rough hands and no time to yourself, and that her mother had long ago accepted what marriage to Da had brought her to, and yet still gave in to her flickerings of longing. Da was sour-tempered and grudging and his belly hung over his trousers, and he never wore a collar to his shirt, which grieved his wife.

Elizabeth crept quietly forward to slide the beans into the waiting colander.

'Elizabeth.' Her mother spoke softly.

Her heart jerked. She sensed she was to be told a secret, something that would be intimate between them, and for a few seconds, but which felt like a time out of all time, the secret was suspended there between them, tangible, knowable, shared, but not yet given the form of words. There was an absolute afternoon stillness, among the canes and the greenness.

'Have you to do any homework?' Her mother

turned away, breaking the invisible thread, evading her eye, and Elizabeth felt herself pushed back again into childhood.

All over the fence and the broken-down wall, the nasturtiums blazed.

She liked it best in winter, with early dark, and the wood fire on, and she and her mother and Milo at the table. But that was unimaginable now; winter was a fairy story. They sat out on the back step, and the air was full of midges and cruising wasps, and Milo was off down to the brook. Da would not be back until dark.

Thoughts danced like moths in Elizabeth's head.

'You should travel to other countries, in your years to come. There's a world beyond yourself you must break through to. Never forget it.'

Sometimes her mother would talk like this without any warning – not of clean clothes and homework books, but of adult life and death.

'You should see all there is to be seen.'

She might as well have said, fly to the moon.

'It would be a disappointment to me, Elizabeth, were you not to, and a sad waste.'

Such talk made her uncomfortable, as if she itched

inside her skin. She could not imagine her own future in this place called 'the world'; she only ever went down inside herself – her whole life looked inwards.

'Would I have to?' She picked anxiously at the skin around her bare toes, imagining some ceremony of being cast out, and a terrible solitude among strangers.

'There will be as little for you here as there has been for me. Besides, you will want it.'

No, she would have said. But did not, being unable to explain, even to herself.

The sky was damson-stained by the time the truck clattered in. Hearing it, she remembered Minchy Fagin.

The cocoa was frothing out of the pan. She was to remember it, marrying the image of it to his sudden, extravagant words for ever.

'I'm taking us to the sea. Throw everything up, school and all. We're going.'

Her mother's hand only just hesitated as she was pouring, but Elizabeth saw her eyes flicker anxiously to his face. He was expansive like this, full of schemes and plans, when he'd been with Nolan and Glinty and the rest, drinking.

'A week in this weather would about set us all up.'

Tiny bubbles prickled over the surface of the cocoa.

They were hustled upstairs, so that she knew he had not said anything about it before now, and that Ma was waiting until they were out of the way, to get at the truth of it.

'Will it be fishing? Will it be sea, to swim in? Will we sleep out on the sand all night?'

'Hush, you.'

She set her hand in the small of her brother's back, going behind him up the stairs. She did not want to talk about it, not until all possibility of disappointment was past. She thought of the sea, curling over her bare feet.

'He said a whole week, Elizabeth. You heard, didn't you? He said it was to be a week. Elizabeth, why won't you say anything?'

'It might not happen. There might not be the money.'

'It will. It will . . . and Minchy Fagin won't be

going to the sea. Minchy Fagin doesn't know anything at all.' His face was lit with hope.

They went the next morning, all of them in a line along the front seat of the truck.

'It's education in itself,' Da had said, answering their mother's disapproval of the missing school time.

'And where's the use of the half they do? Tell me that. We'll stop off for a fish supper as well.' And he had lifted his hands from the wheel, while they were going along, smacked and rubbed them together, and all the time casting a sideways glance at Ma, who had firmed her lips, but kept the words back, knowing him in this mood, and too proud to nag.

But there was no fish supper. She had packed sandwiches and buns, and they ate them going along. Da dropping egg and tomatoes down his shirt front, anyhow and deliberately, Elizabeth knew, because Ma had defied him with her sense, and taken the extravagant pleasure out of the fish supper.

And then, they were there. The truck turned without any warning off the road, through a gap in the hedge, and bumped over grass, and stopped, and a cow loomed its great, square head at the truck window. But they were used enough to cows.

Later, she thought of her mother's feelings at arriving in a field full of cowpats, and thistles like spears, to a caravan that smelled of rustiness and mice. Years later, when it was all over, she understood how it had been, with a senseless man who had no notion of your real needs, but who was given to such fits of craziness, taking you five miles from the nearest house, and a half-mile to a tap, when you had already been threatened with losing the pregnancy no one knew you had.

Later, she saw how Ma's life had been for fifteen years, nothing but a round of work and disappointment, with, just occasionally, ten minutes to sit on the step with her face to the sun. Later, when Elizabeth herself looked at some boy with a new haircut raw up his neck, and eyes glistening with nervous lust, she thought of it, and the thought was enough to draw her sharply back into herself.

Later. But not tonight, when she was drooping tired, yet too excited to sleep, nor the next morning, when she woke to a milky light, and the soft sough and rasp of the sea, dragging down the shingle.

The bed was a plank, with a thin, sour mattress, and both of the windows were partly broken, so that sometime between sleep and now, she had been aware of the cow's breath on her face, and of Ma crying quietly.

When she stepped outside, entirely by herself, she had looked straight over the edge of the world, onto the shining sea, and she ran on bare feet towards it, arms open.

They were there four days before it happened, and the sun never stopped shining, but there was always a wonderful coolness off the sea. Milo leaped about like a goat-kid, wild and solitary, talking to himself.

There was no warning. Elizabeth sat up in the middle of the fifth night, wakened by odd, half-smothered moans and whisperings and the torch waving over the walls and roof like a drunken thing. It caught Milo's face, and his eyes were huge and terrified in the light of it.

'Your Ma's in trouble. You stay with her, Elizabeth. You stay here.' He was dragging on his trousers.

'No. I want to come with you. I don't want to be left.'

'Jesus, girl, you do as you're told just the once, why can't you?'

The injustice stung even then, in the midst of it all. She had never disobeyed him, never dared. Then he went out into the darkness, dragging Milo down the step after him, and away towards the truck.

For a moment, it was utterly still and silent. She crouched back in her bunk against the wall, and prayed to God.

'Elizabeth? Elizabeth, be a good girl. Light the lamp. He's taken the torch with him.'

'Yes.'

'You turn up the oil with the little knob.'

'Yes.'

'I don't like to be in the dark.'

The lamp flared and then sank back to a low blue flicker.

'Will you come here and sit by me?'

She reached out. Ma's hand was slippery and hot.

'Minchy Fagin said you'd been to see the doctor.'

'Minchy Fagin!'

A breeze blew through the broken window-pane, making the lamp sputter.

'Da's gone for someone. He took Milo with him.'

Her mother gave a sudden, sharp cry.

'He'll bring the doctor back, won't he?'

'The dear knows. How'll he find me one, Elizabeth? I don't know.' She was gripping Elizabeth's hand; the nails were sharp.

'Should I get you a drink of water?'

'No, no.'

'What should I do?' She was afraid. She wanted to be anywhere, for things to be normal again, for someone else to be here.

'He met a man who had this place to let. Why did he waste his money on a tin shack in the middle of nowhere? Because he has no sense.'

Elizabeth wanted to stop her ears.

'You shouldn't think of yourself, they say, you should always put others first. You should never be self-regarding.'

'I know.' Though she had always questioned it, for what other person did she, Elizabeth, know, so well as she knew her own self? What other point of reference had she? How else might she measure the truth of things than against herself? If she denied and obliterated this Elizabeth, what was left?

'Don't listen to it, don't! Don't make that mistake, Elizabeth.'

She thought, let them come back, let them bring

163

someone quickly. I don't want this. Her mother was crying, and then stifling her cries in the blanket, and Elizabeth's hand was held stuffed hard against her mouth. She felt her mother's teeth biting into her in pain.

'But it was for you to have this time. A week by the sea. That was all.'

And they had, running across the hot shingle to the water, hearing the hiss and lap of the waves through the darkness.

'It won't stop, Elizabeth. There's no way I can make it stop.'

She had not understood then, not until later, after Da had come back, with a woman who was the only help he could find. She had been some kind of nurse, she said, though way back.

There had never been a chance for her, the woman had said, not a chance, the poor girl, the blood and all had soaked through the mattress to the floor below.

Elizabeth had gone to the truck, shaking, and climbed in, and sat there with Milo, who was fallen asleep across the seats. She had moved him to be closer to her, and seen the torch flickering about inside the caravan. But after a time, she had slept, too, and when she had woken, it was light, and there was an ambulance and a black car drawn up beside the caravan. Da had been standing out there, helplessly, in the field, shirtless.

A terrible knowledge shocked her through. She remembered the feel of Ma's hand, and the fear in her voice that had sounded like complaining, as they had sat together, and that had been in another life. Now, she knew at once, in this cold dawn, that she must set herself aside, as her mother had done. Her arm was numb beneath Milo's sleeping weight.

Looking up, she saw Da, eyes bleared and wild, seeking her out.

They had simply abandoned the caravan – even left the door swinging open. Their things had been piled anyhow into the truck, without being packed. Elizabeth had felt ashamed of it.

The oil lamp had long since guttered out.

'You'll be away to school again tomorrow.'

Then, they had driven all the way, in silence, with Milo rigid and white-faced between them, and never once stopped. They could pee when they got home, Da said, and they had not dared to question it.

When the truck slewed onto the rough ground at the back of the house, the late afternoon sun was slanting through the bean canes. Elizabeth saw Ma there, picking in the green, undersea light. She wanted to duck down and swim to her, and she could not.

But it was Da who leaned his head on the steering wheel of the truck then, took in a great breath and let it out again in one single, juddering, lurching sob.

Milo had not let go her hand for the whole journey, and would not now, and so she sat, trapped there between them.

'Go in, Elizabeth. The stove's not lit. You'll have to get the sticks.'

But still, for a long time, she did not move, only sat, not able to let her grief out, and the truth in. Not wanting the future to begin with this one, simple act, of obeying him.

The brooch

The brooch

The remarkable thing was that so many people did not know he was blind. That was his pride, her aunt Elsa said.

'You must never, by word or deed, show that you know it.'

She had repeated the words to herself, at the same time pinching her nails hard into her palms. They had come on the train, in a compartment smelling of the oranges a woman opposite had taken out of her bag and peeled, onto a handkerchief.

Eating in public was common, her mother said. The child's head was crammed with their sayings, like buttons packed into a box. Years later, on a walk, or serving a customer across the counter, one would come to her unbidden, as if someone moving things about in an attic had disturbed the box, and it had come open and spilled about.

In this way a memory of her uncle would return, and of her aunt Elsa, who had to inject herself twice a day in the thigh, because she was diabetic. She had once come upon her in the bathroom, extending a stringy, blue-veined leg.

Later there had been whispering.

'Don't let the child see.'

'It's life. You cannot keep things from her.'

'Dolly is over-protective,' the aunt said. Dolly was the family name. In their own world, her mother called herself Dora.

'Dolly is over-protective with that child.' (Whose own name was Rima, after a girl in a book.)

And so, getting out of the train, bearing the smell of the oranges faintly on her coat, she remembered. 'Never, by any word or deed.'

But it was a remarkable story. She understood that later. He had been struck blind on the instant, after what they called a brain-storm, at the age of eighteen and so had had to give up his job in an accounting office. He had a genius for figures, a genius and a passion, figures fascinated him, he told the child, you could play with figures like toys, but better, because you grew out of toys. Walking down the long avenue between the bungalows, or across the flat, flat sands that went on for ever to the flatter sea, the dog let off the lead to run ahead, he shot figures at her like bullets.

'Five nines?'

'Seven add seven, divided by seven?'

'A tenth of a thousand? Of a hundred? Of a tenth?'

'One six is six, two sixes are twelve, three sixes are . . . ?'

'Listen to this. Every part of the nine times table adds together to make nine. Two nines are eighteen – one, add eight, is nine. Three nines are twenty-seven – two, add seven, makes nine. Four nines are?'

'Thirty-six.'

'Three and six make?'

'Nine.'

'That's the beauty of it.'

And he shouted suddenly, and waved his stick in triumph to the sky. (It was not a white stick.)

'That's the beauty.'

'Look,' she said, and stopped to stare down at her own footmarks that pressed into the sand and at once filled up with water, and the water reflected the sky. And then the footprints sank back into the sand again with a tiny sucking sound.

'Look.' That was beauty, to her. 'Look!'

He came back. Looked down. And her face burned, in the realisation of what she had said. 'Look.' And that he could not.

'Never by one word or deed.' So she could not apologise, could not refer to it in any way. But she put her hand into his as they walked.

The dog Shep ran up and down, far out at the water's edge, barking after seagulls.

He could never have sat at home idle, his mother had seen to that, and his own determination. By the time he had met Elsa – who had gone to a Ladies' Night at the Masonic with her father, because her mother had felt unwell – his new way of life was established, and taken for granted by everyone. His blindness had not troubled Elsa. She had ignored it. Already, plenty of people did not know that he was blind, but those who did would marvel.

He had become a commercial traveller in hosiery, with a leather attaché case crammed full of samples – men's socks, and children's, and ladies' stockings in every shade and gauge. By the time he and Elsa married, his routine was set and he had only to move it, along with his things, out of his parents' house and into his own, which was the bungalow that Elsa's father had built for them.

The alarm clock was set for six every morning, because he did things so slowly. He made a pot of tea, each action following the next in the same, methodical routine, and took a cup, with an arrowroot biscuit, in to Elsa, who needed to eat and drink on waking, because of her diabetes. After that, and her own routine of the injection, she waited on him, cooking breakfast, brushing his coat and trilby hat, polishing his shoes and setting them out beside the front door. He sat down at the table on the signal of the pips for seven o'clock, and the news on the wireless. They ate as they listened, and then she went through the suitcase with him, listing the contents, and the exact order in which they were arranged, and he stood beside her and memorised each item, touching his hand briefly to it, and then the case was closed and at the snap of the lock, the dog, Gem, or Shep, or Ben, a series of identical sheepdogs, who replaced one another over forty years, would jump up and go to the front door, to wait, expectant, eager.

'You could set the clock by Mr Burgage,' they said. The child heard it often enough.

The walk to the railway station took him fourteen minutes. At the triangular kiosk on the corner the newsagent waited, holding out the *Daily Telegraph* to his reaching hand, and at the marble horse-trough they paused for the dog to drink, and every morning was like every other morning, and nothing varied.

He caught the seven-fifty, with a season ticket, and held the newspaper up to his face, turning the pages as the other men did, and the other men never knew. Or so it was believed.

In the city the dog led, crossing at traffic junctions, turning on a command – for he held the map of the place in his head, together with the list of his calls in their order, and at every shop and department store he was punctual, for the time ticked within him like a second heart. He set out his samples and displayed the socks and stockings by stretching them carefully over his hand.

'Burnt sand,' he said. 'Camel', 'Blush', 'Regulation Navy', 'Waverley – a more subtle blue.' He remembered the words of colours, but no one could know whether what he saw within, behind his sightlessness, in any way corresponded now to the reality, whether blue was indeed blue.

They gave him the orders. 'One dozen grey gents' half-hose. Size 9–11. Two dozen navy. Size eight. A dozen boys', aged nine to ten. Fifty pairs of thirty denier, seam-free. Fifty pairs of silk sheer, Blush. Medium.' Trainees, new to hosiery, would remark that Mr Burgage never took out an order book, never wrote anything down at all in any way, but the question that might have followed was not asked – though later, in the staff cloakroom, they might whisper among themselves. And it was remarkable, for no order was ever wrong, there was never a mistake.

The evening paper was handed to him by another seller, on another corner, but this one he did not open on the train, it was carried home pristine and unfolded, for Elsa, and given to the dog as they reached the gate, to carry in to her.

In the bungalow the routine was always the same. The names and the figures waited, arranged as they had been entered, in the order book of his head. She had a tray of tea ready, and he drank two cups at once, and set a third on the arm of the chair; then, he began to speak, head back against the moquette, lids half-closed over unfocused eyes. The order was transferred, in Elsa's oblique writing, onto the pad.

'One dozen grey gents' half-hose. Size 9–11. Two dozen navy. Size eight. A dozen boys', aged nine to ten. Fifty pairs of thirty denier, seam-free. Fifty pairs of silk sheer. Blush. Medium.' His concentration must not be interrupted, the child had been told, she must never speak a word during this time, never distract either of them or the order would fall into disorder, the figures fly about anyhow from his head to Elsa's page and never be correctly rearranged again. And so she would sit under the dining table, her own legs pressed against the dark wooden legs, or else behind the sofa holding a book. But she was never reading, only listening, listening. 'One dozen grey gents' half-hose, size eleven. Two dozen navy, size 9–11.'

In forty years his routine had not altered. In forty years, it was said, he had never made a mistake.

On Friday nights he went to the Masonic Lodge.

'Never ask questions. Never speak to him about it,' the child was told. 'Those are secret matters.'

They walked on the beach to a point parallel with the seafront houses, and then turned, and he knew precisely where to turn, she did not have to stop or prompt him, which was a miracle to her, and yet, by now, one that was quite taken for granted. The dog went on running about at the edge of the water, busy with seagulls, though it turned when they did and ran about again, going the other way, and the sea never came nearer. People rode racehorses through the shallows.

He talked to her. He was always gnawing over something, Elsa said. Why men wanted to fly – how it had always been an instinct, an impossible, physical desire, how they had flown in dreams, and legend and early art. Whether there was really any such thing as the Blood Royal. What was the point or purpose of the migration of hirondines. He taught her to pronounce the word carefully – 'Hirondine'.

'A wonder of the world, some would say, and proof as to the existence of a Creator.' He had stopped and begun to dig a neat little hole in the sand with the ferrule of his stick. 'It seems to me no such thing.' She went close and looked down, as the hole filled up with water.

'Think of the waste.' He turned on her so that she started. She tried to see into his eyes, which were looking about anyhow, wildly, in his anger.

'A waste of effort, without any point or purpose. See those sand worms?' The ferrule dabbed down, here and there, pointing at the small, grainy coils. To her that was a proof, the fact that he knew their whereabouts exactly, sightlessly.

The wind blew, ripping hard over the open sand, and the dog came running in towards them.

At Pitt's Café, they always had the same order, and that was another ritual – a slice of apple pie and a slice of treacle tart, a pot of tea, a milky cocoa, and a bowl of water for the dog. She slipped the pie crust to it under the table, feeling the slippery nose and mouth cold against her fingers.

'Your aunt doesn't know about this, and your mother would call it very common.' She waited for him to tap the side of his nose and to wink, an odd, clumsy wink that did not completely come down over his eye. Then, across the green plastic table, she would try again to look into his eyes, at the milky surface which was faded and grey. The eyes never focused on her; there was no one there. She did not understand how people were said not to know about the blindness.

'What are you staring at?'

The brooch

They left, taking a snicket between the café and the public conveniences, back towards the town. She came four times a year, with the seasons, and they took the same way whatever the weather, and the only difference was that in December and April, they saw no one else, and the sands were pale and bare as a desert, under the enormous sky.

The last time came abruptly. It was October. The dog was called Shep, and the best one ever, he said. The seagulls were strung out like pearls along the water's edge, hundreds of them, and Shep raced to flurry and scatter them.

At first, the week had seemed no different. When they had walked into the bungalow, at five o'clock in the afternoon, it had smelled the same, the smell she dreamed of sometimes when she was at home, an intense, many-layered smell, and each room had a slight variation – in the bathroom, traces of antiseptic from the solution in which Elsa's syringes were steeped, in the front room, a faint staleness, and the clothiness of the moquette.

He came home at twenty past six, the dog Shep running in with the newspaper, and the tea was on the table, and she must be silent. There was the recitation of that day's order.

'Less again,' Elsa said.

He did not reply.

'Weren't you expecting the new samples to have come?'

He did not reply.

Later, she realised that the knowledge of what had happened had been hovering in the air at that moment, and had brushed against her, and that there was an unease in his silence.

'Your books came. Nothing else.'

The books were not ordinary books, they were gramophone recordings that came in flat, heavy boxes, tied with leather straps, and were exchanged for a new set every other week. He listened to them for an hour each evening, and sometimes the child listened with him, to *The History of the Second World War* by Winston Churchill, and the diaries of statesmen, and the lives of kings. Travellers read of journeys and philosophers asked the questions which she herself asked constantly. What is the world? What is real? Who am I? But their answers were intricate, incomprehensible. He listened to the novels of Charles Dickens and Arnold Bennett, and the plays of Shakespeare. When she was not there, he listened alone. Elsa took her book into the stuffiness of the front room, preferring to hear words in silence, in her own head.

The new book was *The Origin of Species*. She stayed listening with him for a short time only. His eyes were closed. She scrutinised his face, the thick folds from nose to chin, and the flesh of his neck; he was a heavy man, and almost bald. She tried to slide the door open soundlessly but it brushed along the carpet.

'Ten tomorrow,' he said. 'All set?'

'All set.'

It would be Saturday. 'All set' was what they always said.

But it was different, from the beginning, though she could not say why. There was simply an unease.

The sun shone, reflecting on the flat surface of the water, and there was a little warmth in it. He talked, but not as usual; today, there were not the problems about the ordering of the universe. Instead, he spoke in odd, disjointed sentences, about trivial things.

'Arthur Jenkins – he travels up on the same train,

same compartment, wife's a sister of the Grand Master. Arthur Jenkins dropped his spectacles on the rails, down the edge of the platform. They held us up for fifteen minutes, but they fished them out, do you know. Shep has fleas. Do you think Shep has fleas? Better get some powder. Better tell your aunt, she can't stand a dog that scratches. Do you know that tea-set, the one with the tree – "Tree of Life", they call the design? She was given that, on a Masonic Ladies' night. We look after the wives. Marry into the Masons and you'll be taken care of. She's no need to worry. Do they use lard or margarine, for the pastry in these pies? It tasted of lard the last time. It's different today. My mother would never have anything but butter. I wonder they use lard. Could be pork lard, and they do have Jews in. Do you know about Jews? Jews have been some of my best customers.'

After they had eaten at the café, they always went back to the bungalow over the level crossing, where they waited by the gates for the London train to go through. The only people they saw were in the shops of the Parade, where they went if the aunt had given them an errand. But today was different. There was a tight, pinching feeling inside her.

Walking beside him towards the town, along back streets she did not know, away from the level crossing and the Parade, she avoided the cracks in the paving slabs with particular care. The voice in her head asked, What is life? Is it a waste of effort that birds migrate? What are light and darkness? When I am dead, will I know it?

The week had not been the same.

The dog Shep was uncertain here and did not trot ahead, and once the uncle confused the way, so that they found themselves on wasteground near the coal tips.

'Drunk again,' he said. They doubled back.

There was a door in the side of a warehouse they came to, with an engraved plate. She had not liked the change in their routine, and the feeling she had within her now was fear.

'Elsa has that dressing-table set, the comb and brushes and mirror, with the mother-of-pearl backs. You know them. They're very high quality. They came from here.'

A cubby-hole office with glass sides looked into the

body of the warehouse, which had metal shelving like Meccano, stacked with boxes, and crates on the floor.

'This friend's a Jew.'

She wondered what a Jew would be, but he was just a man like any other, small, with a moustache and an overall the colour of cardboard.

'This is the young lady,' the uncle said. The man put out his hand to her to shake, and as she did so, in that precise moment she felt that the world took a lurch forward, pushing her closer to adult life. She was like a snake inside the beginnings of a new skin, and the strangeness of it troubled her.

She was to choose a present for herself. That was why they were here. A chair with a hooped back was set for her, and then trays of jewellery came out, brooches and necklaces and small bangles and pins, attached to black velvet pads.

She was completely free to choose.

The dog Shep lapped noisily from the dish of water they had brought.

There were questions she could not ask. Why were they here, now, today, to give her a present? How should she choose? How much was the present to cost? And what her mother would say bubbled inside her head.

'Expensive presents are always bribes.'

'No one can buy affection.'

'Jewellery that draws attention to itself is vulgar.'

The things were of emeralds and sapphires, silver and gold. But what she liked best and wanted she had seen at once. It was a brooch of a small poodle dog, with a sparkling body of diamonds and studded red rubies in a pattern for the collar and the eyes.

'Take your time,' he said. They were talking, and out of politeness, she looked at other brooches, at a bracelet, beaded with coral, and a pearl rose pin, resting on her palm. But she wanted the diamond dog.

'Has that caught the young lady's fancy? The little doggy brooch?'

Hearing it, and feeling her own flush of immediate anger at the words, addressed as if to a baby, she knew that she had been right, that things were different, and she was no longer a child.

She stood up. The brooch lay apart from the rest of the jewellery, on the table, the ruby eye gleaming as the sun caught it, through the skylight.

'We seem to have made our selection.'

She loathed him. He was on one side, and she and the uncle on another.

'Dolly has always been proud,' Elsa had once said. She understood what it meant now.

He picked up the brooch.

'Very nice choice,' he said, 'very suitable,' and held it up, not to her, but in front of her uncle's face.

'Isn't that pretty? Isn't that a nice choice for a young lady? See? Can you see it at all?' He pushed it right up, under the uncle's nose.

So it was not true that people did not know. The blindness was obvious, she saw that now.

'Very nice,' he said. 'Very nice.'

The place was hateful to her, suffocating, she wanted to be outside. But they must wait for the brooch to be put into a padded box, and the box wrapped and tied with fine string and made into a little handle, which the man set to dangle on her forefinger, and that was how she carried it, holding it up so that it swung a little.

It had begun to rain. In the alleyway leading from the warehouse the cobblestones were greasy. She wanted to thank him, but for a moment could not speak, only held the parcel, and felt disbelief that it contained the diamond dog with the ruby collar and eyes, and that the dog was hers. He fumbled with his stick and Shep's lead. The rain beaded the sleeves of his coat and the beads gleamed.

'The dog brooch is so beautiful.' She heard her own voice sounding odd, clear and high and formal, as if she were speaking to a stranger, some friend of her mother to whom she must be polite.

'Thank you very much indeed for giving it to me.'

They stood, Shep close between them so that she smelled the doggy smell that came off him as the rain soaked his coat. Then she looked up.

He was crying. It was not the rain. Tears were coming quite silently out of the sightless eyes and running down his fleshy, fallen cheeks.

He said, 'I'm a cast-off. On the scrap heap. That's the bottom of it. I haven't told Elsa. I'm telling you.'

She was silent, not fully understanding, and yet appalled.

'Out,' he said, and made a gesture with his arm. 'I'm out.'

The rain was soaking her hair and neck, cold, bitter rain. The dog pressed closer and whimpered slightly.

Behind them, the lamps set along the warehouse came on suddenly.

Then she knew that it had indeed been different, and why. It was the last time. He had no more work. They had asked him to go. The routine of his daily life was finished. She did not know why this should make any difference to their walks on the beach, and the pies and tea and cocoa in the café, the wait to see the London train by the level crossing. That routine had nothing to do with his weekday work. But they would not go again, she knew, and the next time she came here she would be older. She was already older. That was why he had bought her the brooch.

'Wait a minute, please,' she said and, sheltering beneath the overhang of the warehouse roof, with the drops of rain rolling off it onto her shoulders, she unpicked the string handle with her fingernails, and unwrapped the paper parcel, opened the box. The diamond dog gleamed in the silvery wet afternoon light, and the collar and eyes glinted their rubies. She lifted it out and pinned it on the lapel of her woollen coat. She did not speak. Neither of them spoke, they only turned to go on, up the alleyway, the dog Shep pulling on the lead. And then, suddenly, she was afraid, because it was the end of things, because she felt unlike herself. The ground was no longer firm beneath her. She wanted to be home, wanted warmth and to be as she had been, secure inside her old, unchanged self, wanted to be dried and petted and given hot tea, and hear some strange, sonorous voice reading from the gramophone.

In the last long avenue, she took hold of his hand. But when they reached the bungalow, they were met with anger, because he had kept her out for so long, and it was growing dark and they were soaking wet from the rain.

And when she showed the brooch on the lapel of her brown coat, her mother's face pursed up in disapproval. The dog was not diamonds and the collar and eyes were not rubies. It was diamanté only, and that was common, her mother said, and quite unsuitable to give to a child.

Antonyin's

Antonyin's

He was one of the few people who could have felt a lift of heart on seeing the buildings at Vldansk. They were ugly, and yet to him they were — not beautiful, but something that was higher than beauty: they were perfectly symmetrical. From every angle, they satisfied, but particularly on first approach, driving up the wide avenue set with fir trees regularly spaced, and he was stilled and settled by the sight of them. He would be contented here. That was now certain. Others who might have come had attachments and commitments, or did not want to put themselves out of sight and the chance of promotion. He was unattached, with only himself to satisfy, and he found his work of consuming interest. The prospect of the coming year excited him.

There was nothing else to be enjoyed in Vldansk. The city was without charm or idiosyncrasy, raw and with no sense of a past. The oldest feature was an ornate and hideous marble horse trough, with winged warriors rearing from the sides and dating from just before the First World War. In summer horses still drank from it – they were in general use here, not only on the miles of flat surrounding fields, but in the streets themselves, pulling vegetable carts, bringing farmers into town, among the grey, sardine-can cars.

For three weeks he lived in a hotel until the company flat was made ready for him. There was life in the place to make up for the flat beer and greasy, gristly sausages, the coarse blankets, and peculiar-smelling soap that came in little, rough sticks. When he moved into the apartment, it felt as dead as the surface of the moon. The four blocks were set down at right angles to one another, on a featureless road three miles out of the town, without any neighbour-hood streets or meeting places, and completely surrounded by turnip fields, which when he arrived, were being harvested. For two weeks, the carts moved slowly up and down the rows, and there was the sight of men lifting the vegetables and slashing their tops, before hurling them up into the wagons. The horses stood, chewing on mangy-looking hay. The turnip smell, like that of unwashed feet, seeped into the flat and lingered there.

But the activity was something to look at, each morning. At the end of the second week, the fields and sky were bright with bonfires, and the ground itself was set on fire, the flames running this way and that across it like tracers across the night sky. The firing was like some sort of festival. The workers brought their families, riding out on the carts and in dilapidated old vans and on an army of bicycles, and their children danced wild demoniacal dances in the light of the flames. The acrid smell of smoke drove out the vegetal gases at last.

The next day, the fields were charred and still smoking, but by eleven, rain had come and damped the fires out, and with them, whatever life there had fleetingly been. After that, autumn merged into the beginning of winter, and deadness everywhere. Nothing moved on the fields save for a hare which he saw once or twice racing across the barren brown furrows. When the first frosts, and then the snow came, it, too, was gone.

But at least the snowfall brought a brightness. He lay in bed seeing the pale sheen on the ceiling the first morning after it had fallen, and when he opened the curtains his spirits lifted at the whiteness, where there had been only grey and dun. But after a while, the sight of the snow became tedious too, and he began to feel starved of colour, to crave it, in this monochrome world, he dreamed of colour, of the Mediterranean and California, sunlit, garish, technicolour places. Even people's clothes and skin were colourless here.

But he was not unhappy. He cycled to work, leaving at seven, when it was still dark. On three evenings, he had a language lesson; a fat woman whose breath and hair and clothes reeked of onion, came to the works to teach him, in one of the empty offices under the weird, flickering neon strip-light. The language was impossible, guttural and harsh, with a complex grammar. She was not a good teacher. And so, they seemed locked together like wrestlers over the impenetrable words. Outside the windows, the snow fell and fell, mesmerising him.

On the other evenings he almost always went into the town, to sit in the hotel bars, not seeking company or conversation, but merely to look at the stir of life around him.

He discovered Antonyin's by chance. The food of the country was unappetising, and sometimes disgusting; he had often to spit out lumps of unidentifiable, gristly meat. The vegetables, onions, green or red cabbage, turnip and swede only, were hard and unsalted, and glutinous dumplings floated in every dish. He felt himself growing bloated, his bowels were irregular, his stomach felt gassy, and his mouth tasted permanently of grease. Then, he would simply stop eating, sometimes for days on end, though he drank a great deal of peppermint and lemon tea, and chewed liquorice root, until hunger got the better of him and he was forced back to the food again. Once, he bought a huge tin of condensed milk from a market stall and ate it late at night, spooning it up directly from the can.

His hair grew onto his collar and he went to a barber who clipped it to a raw stubble, high up his neck. His teeth ached and he dared not visit a dentist. He had boils.

Yet still he was not unhappy. He made no friends, but his conversations with some of those who spoke English were pleasant enough and one afternoon, when he had been in semi-starvation for several days, and his stomach rumbled, one of his colleagues remarked that it was clear he had not yet discovered Antonyin's.

'The food there won't give you the gripes, at any rate.'

A few days later, finding that they had dug up the pavement outside one of the hotels, he had to take a back route, turned up an unfamiliar alleyway, and became lost. It was then that he found Antonyin's. He might have walked straight past, it was so unprepossessing. Three steps led down to the door, and a blur of smoke and steam obscured the room beyond. But he could make out the sign over the window. 'Antonyin.'

He was never to forget the first time he opened the door onto the crowded café, the first time that blast of air hit him, as if he had lifted the lid of a great bubbling cauldron, never to forget the smells — cooking oil and black tobacco, beer, spices, men's sweat, and the ubiquitous, sweetish hair-oil.

That night, it was as if he were tasting food for the first time. There was no menu, no choice. The hotels and other eating places made a great show of offering a huge variety, but in practice most things were permanently unavailable. In any case, whatever there was tasted the same.

He was served with some crisply fried fish, a bowl

of thickly caramelised onion soup and a stew of what might have been hare, with buttered noodles and spiced red cabbage. The richness of the spices, the tenderness of the meat and perfectly cooked vegetables, lifted the everyday peasant ingredients into another class. He wiped his plate with a slice of bread, fresh, coarse-textured and moist, nothing like the sour grey stuff he had grown used to.

Around him, men were smoking and talking, drinking beer and schnapps. He felt separate from them, but not at all unwelcome, not a stranger, though he heard no word of English. He cycled back to the apartment proofed and warm against the bitter wind by the good food inside him, but more, by a feeling of having finally broken through some barrier to the close, inner heart of this bleak city, where there was warmth, conviviality and colour.

After that he went to Antonyin's almost every night, so that his body began to grow replete, to be smooth and solid again, no longer bloated with dough and grease.

The woman came into the café on a freezing night in December, and sat down not far from him. At first, he was not particularly conscious of her, though the fact that she *was* a woman marked her out in a place where, the wife of the proprietor who waited on them apart, no woman came. When she returned on the following night, and again alone, he noted her, and saw that she stared at him.

By now he was a regular. The proprietor greeted him as 'Englishman'. He was happy there. One night he was invited to join a card game, and though the attempt was abandoned as the playing became too fast and argumentative for him to follow, he sat drinking his coffee and watching, trying to decipher what was being said in the thick local accents.

The food was always wonderful; sometimes there was a joint of roast meat, boar or pork, or venison. One night a miraculous pudding appeared, treacle-dark and stuffed with prunes and raisins. But even when soup and stew were the same every night for a week, the subtle changes of herbs or seasoning meant there was no monotony.

A week after her first appearance there, the woman came in and straight away sat down at his table. She was ugly, in a half-repulsive, half-fascinating way, small, with a short thick neck that seemed to sink down between her shoulders, and prominent eyes, whose lashes were oddly pale, like those of an albino. Her skin, soft and clear as a young child's, was pale too. He could not have guessed her age.

'Englishman.'

He nodded slightly.

'I have waited to speak to you.'

Behind her head, he saw through the window that it had begun to snow again. He should leave, to begin the slow cycle ride home.

'I have wanted to tell you my life.'

She gave off the smell of desperation. As she talked, he felt the energy begin to drain out of him, so that after a while, he could have laid his head on the wooden table and slept there. But he did not sleep. He listened, and the pale, protuberant eyes stared, stared at him.

She had been brought up in a small town on the coast. Her father had been a deep-sea fisherman, a harsh illiterate man, who had severed a leg in some hauling equipment, and then been obliged to sit at home, or else limp about the quayside, boiling with rage and resentment.

When she was eleven her mother had died, of weariness and disappointment as much as from any physical cause, and the girl, the oldest of six children, had been expected to take her place. Some genetic flaw had caused her grotesque physical appearance, the slightly misshapen body, and the protuberant eyes and peculiar paleness – she spoke of it detachedly, as if she were a doctor discussing a mildly interesting case.

At fifteen she had left home and come to Vldansk to find work in a tailoring shop. She had planned to send for her sister, but the girl had died of pneumonia that winter, after she had left.

'The boys went to sea,' she said, 'then my father drowned. He fell off the quay. It might have been an accident.'

He could detect neither sadness nor longing for her lost family, for the past and her childhood. She spoke of it as if it was someone else's history.

He was uneasy and embarrassed, yet felt obliged to humour her by staying to listen. His deep pleasure in the evenings at Antonyin's was soured and he began to be anxious every time he came down the dingy little street to the café door. If he opened it and she was not yet there his spirits lifted, and he called out cheerfully to the other regulars. When she came in he felt oppressed, and the evening was drained of any enjoyment. Annoyed that it should be so, and at her hold over him, he kept away from the café for over a week, stayed late at work, then went straight back to the flat, with bread and cheese and a few pickled herrings, bought from the market. He struggled with his language primer, or read, without real interest, from the odd selection of English books left over the years on an office shelf.

He returned to Antonyin's out of defiance. He missed the food, and the close, comforting atmosphere. He would not be driven away to live like a rat in a hole. She was not there, and on a tide of relief and high spirits he drank too much, for the first time since coming to Vldansk; in any case, that was something he had almost never done. He was a controlled man.

After that, he went away for nearly three weeks, visiting mines and oil fields five hundred miles away to the east, in a part of the country where it scarcely came light all day, and the wind hurled and battered at him until he thought he might go mad. The people were pinched, sour, inward-turned, and he had difficulty in understanding their harsh regional accent.

Vldansk seemed lively and welcoming, and he returned to its now familiar streets with a sense of joy, as if returning home. But it was to Antonyin's that he looked to complete his sense of homecoming. He would buy everyone a beer; his return would be a celebration.

He saw her at once, through the cloud of steam and smoke. She was sitting in the far corner and her eyes were on him the moment he stepped through the door. He went to the far side of the room from her. Why not? He did not know her. He was under no obligation.

She came to his table as the soup arrived, shuffling onto the wooden bench and then leaning against the wall and watching his face intently, every time he raised the spoon to drink. It was onion soup again, dark and thick, with skeins of cheese stringing across the surface. He ate it too fast, while it was hot, so that tears came to his eyes. She went on staring. There was a dish of sour green pickles on the table, and now and then she put one in her mouth. He was angry. He resented her. The evening was spoiled.

'What do you want with me?' He set down his

spoon in the empty bowl. He had scarcely ever spoken to her. She had been the one who had talked.

'What do you want?'

'Marriage.'

She might have said 'stew' or 'coffee' or even 'money'.

'Marriage.'

At the other end of the café, a great roar of laughter went up from a group of men, and fists drummed briefly on the table. His empty soup bowl was taken away, and a dish of the usual stew set down; hot sage and paprika smelled earthy in the steam that rose from it.

He broke his bread into lumps. He was appalled. He thought of simply abandoning the food and walking out. Then she began to stare at him again out of the protuberant eyes.

She had planned it, thought out every detail with care. She had plenty of time to think while she worked, she said, and then alone in her flat in the evenings. The idea had come to her months ago, and every day, she had gone most carefully over it. She did not want a husband to live with — she shook her head in scorn. She'd seen enough of husbands, at home, and here, among her work companions and neighbours. Husbands were no good; they were either bad-tempered, demanding and often cruel, or else they were 'just great lumps'. She wanted to get away. There was no good future for her here in Vldansk, only years of tailoring and loneliness, stretching towards old age. The idea of arranging a marriage for herself had come to her as her one hope of escape. She would find an Englishman, or an American, one of those who came to work in the city from time to time, as he had, and go back with him, to be married but then leave him at once, and begin a new, independent life of her own.

'Others have done it,' she said simply. 'Why not me? Why should I not?'

He felt himself begin to sweat so much that the inside of his collar became wet, and his shirt stuck to his back. He wiped his sleeve across his forehead. The close heat of the café, and the hot spiciness of the food he had shovelled into himself so quickly were partly to blame. But mostly, he sweated at what she was saying to him, at the ludicrousness, the enormity of the suggestion, and the impossibility of dealing with it.

'There would be no difficulty. We wait until June. We travel together. In England – in London or else in some other place – you would choose – we would marry. By an official, not by a priest – by a priest would not be right. And then, we part. What could be more simple?'

There was the cool appearance of rationality as well as the obstinacy of the mad about her. She knew. She would have an answer for his every possible objection, and a counter-argument. He foresaw that.

Why should he argue? He would not even discuss the matter. There was no point. He would not do it. The whole notion was repellent, and disgusted him. It was impossible. He felt almost violent about it.

She was sitting quite calmly, stirring her coffee and rum, in no hurry. She had a wart beneath her chin and another close to her left ear, pink and crinkled like the undersides of small mushrooms. He pushed his chair back roughly and got up from the table, counting out some money as he did so. He felt slippery and uncomfortable with the sweat, yet burning hot inside his clothes.

'What you ask is impossible. Impossible. You must

find someone else – if you can. Or else stay put. Yes – stay put.'

She was made of wax. She did not flicker as he turned and walked quickly out of the café, without speaking again. In the bitter air outside, he still felt the sweat. His hands were trembling.

He did not let it affect his work. But occasionally during the day, she would come into his mind, as if she were always lurking at the back of it, like some temporarily forgotten name, and then he would see her squat stumpy body, and that face. He felt guilty about her, and was furious that he did so. He would not let her drive him away from Antonyin's again for long. He stuck to the apartment for a couple of nights, and the hotel bar for another, but on the next, he went back.

She was not there and did not come. After six days, he began to feel safe. He wished he could ask them, for he was sure they knew her, but embarrassment, and a desire not to tempt fate, kept him silent, even supposing he could have made himself understood, for by mentioning her, he might in some dreadful way conjure her up in reality.

On the following Sunday, she came to the flat. He

knew it was her when the doorbell rang – an incongruous, irritating doorbell which played a sickly little tune. He had been cleaning – the vacuum and brushes were about the floor, and for several moments he stood quite still among them. No one came here and he had scarcely seen his neighbours. But it was not that. He had a terrible sense of the woman's presence, mesmerising, relentless, waiting outside on the landing.

'How did you know where to find me? No one has this address.'

'I have followed after you one night late.'

She wore boots and a long grey coat that seemed to have been cut from stiff felt in the way it stood out from her body.

'There is nothing to be said. I can't agree to your demand. It is not possible, that's all.'

She did not reply, only stood obstinately there so that he had either to shut the door in her face, or let her in.

She sat on the edge of the brown leatherette sofa and talked, not begging or pleading, simply re-telling her history, in a monotonous voice, and then stating again the reasons for wanting to escape from Vldansk,

and her longings for a new life. He paced about the
small room, and then stood at the window looking at
the snow-covered fields, treeless and hedgeless,
stretching away until their edge blurred into the line
of the horizon. He felt her staring at his back. He was
angry. He was afraid. He wondered if he could simply
run out of the flat and away, miles and miles across
the hard-packed snow.

Or if he might kill her.

But after a time she stopped talking and, in a while,
simply went, though for some time after she had gone
the room still seemed to hold the imprint of her
unsmiling, relentless presence. He stood without
putting on the lamp, looking out onto the snow.
There were never any stars here, nor the clear
brightness of moonlight, only a gathering greyness,
once day had leaked out of the sky. He wondered if
she had walked or cycled. Then, so as not to think of
her at all, he found paper and pen and wrote a long
letter to an acquaintance in England, a man with
whom he had been at school and had met by chance
some years later, walking across a piece of wasteland
with a greyhound dog. They were in the same field of

work. He had had no thought of writing to him, or indeed to anyone, before today.

That night he dreamed of her again and again, was angered by it. He did not go to Antonyin's for a week. He found a fish café near the railway station and ate there, and the oil in which the food was fried gave him indigestion.

She was waiting for him one evening as he left the works, standing in the snow in her stiff felt coat, her protuberant eyes fixed upon him. He turned away without acknowledging her, and began to walk quickly to the cycle racks.

'I have made supper. I am a good cook. I will lead you the way there.'

'No.'

'It is near the river. Don't lose me out of your sight or you will not arrive.'

She had a bicycle propped up against the fence, a high-handled old machine on which she looked laughable, a circus figure, small and squat and neckless, the grey coat reaching to her heavy boots.

'No.'

Yet he was curious to know how she lived. And hungry. So then, let her make a fool of herself, let her slave over a cooking pot for him. He felt defiant. He would give her nothing else.

The frozen sleet was driven like pine needles into his face and he struggled to see ahead and keep up with her as she swung round corners and skidded down the alleyways that led to the river.

Her rooms, though they felt cold, were nevertheless as oppressive and stifling to him as her physical presence. There was one small living area, and a sink and cooker behind a curtained partition. She shared a lavatory and bath two floors below with the other tenants. The air on the landing and staircase, as well as in the room itself, was thick with the smell of cooking meat and onions.

He was not a tall man but he felt like a giant lumbering inside the overcrowded space. The chairs, and stools and small tables were draped with pieces of beaded and embroidered fabric, and fabric was pinned to the walls here and there, tiny cushions were piled about and there was a clutter of ornaments, half of them cracked or broken. He imagined her squirrelling all this together, surrounding herself with objects to fill the hollow of her existence. The room made him panic.

She was not a good cook. The meat was tough, the lumps of onion half-raw, and he felt the food settle in the pit of his stomach. She talked of her plan. She would pack everything in tea crates and ship it ahead of her, she said, she could not bear to enter on a new life without her own things. But they themselves would fly to England, where he would arrange the marriage licence at once. This should not take many weeks; her papers were all in order. He found himself arguing about the laws and regulations, the difficulties of her even entering the country.

'It is out of the question. You simply do not understand. It is impossible.'

'For me to come to your country, for me to be married to you, it is all possible.'

'No!'

'Why is it "no"? Why? Why?' She was shouting at him. 'You should do this thing. It is nothing. It will never inconvenience you.'

'No.'

He knew that the crates of dreadful cracked ornaments, and beaded drapes and cushions, would be delivered to his own home, and wait there. That she would unpack them and then they would take over, clouding and blurring the tidiness of his domestic life, making disarray where there was at present spareness and order. She would be at his table, in his kitchen, staring, staring. She would somehow contrive to be married to him and having done so, she would never leave.

'I have no other chance. I am not a young woman. It is the only way to a new life. Why do you deny me?'

This time, he did escape, out of the room and down the dark stairs. He did not look back, and yet he had an image of her which he carried for a long time, standing, white-skinned and squat in a claustrophobic room among the ruins of the awful meal, unsmiling. He had never seen her smile.

She did not follow him, but he heard her, shouting after him down the stairs, and then through the open window, high, screeching, furious accusations.

It took two days for him to leave Vldansk. He pleaded a dangerously sick mother. No one questioned it. During that time, he slunk about like a man on the run, taking a circuitous route from his flat to the works, always at different times. He resented being driven out. But the closest he came to real sadness was during his last hour there when, waiting in the half-empty airport lounge, he thought of Antonyin's, and warmth at remembered happiness spurted up in him.

The food on the plane was the old food of the country, congealed grey gristle in paprika with watery cabbage and sour bread. But he ate it, out of relief at finding himself on his way home alone – for he had dreaded seeing her, waiting for him at the airport, wearing the stiff, long grey coat and staring, staring.

England was mild. A warm, damp wind blew diesel fumes across the tarmac. He felt light-headed, almost happy.

His house was as he had left it, cold, ordered, empty, the curtains falling together just so, the books, spine to spine, exactly placed along the shelves. He closed the door.

And then, a terrible, desperate loneliness fell upon him. Emptiness seemed to ring in his ears with the silence. Her loneliness had been buried in mess and clutter, muffled in cloth. His was laid bare as bone in this space. Only at Antonyin's had they both been able, for an evening here and there, to set it separately aside.

She would not leave his head. He imagined her, seeing through the windows and even the walls of his house, pictured her sitting opposite him at his table, in his chairs. He did not want her. He had hated her.

After a few days, he went out to the newsagent and bought a paper, and several magazines and, returning home, began to go through them for the addresses of agencies who might supply him with a foreign wife.